KI, MASTER OF DEATH

The gunfighter screamed but still managed to get his bloody left hand wrapped around the butt of his gun. Ki drove one of the whirling handles of his *han-kei* into the side of the gunfighter's face with lethal force. The man collapsed on the floor, bone fragments from his crushed skull driving into his brain . . .

Also in the LONE STAR series from Jove

LONGARM AND THE LONE STAR LEGEND
LONE STAR AND THE MOON TRAIL FEUD
LONE STAR AND THE GOLDEN MESA
LONE STAR AND THE RIO GRANDE BANDITS
LONE STAR AND THE BUFFALO HUNTERS
LONE STAR AND THE BIGGEST GUN IN THE WEST
LONE STAR AND THE APACHE WARRIOR
LONE STAR AND THE GOLD MINE WAR
LONE STAR AND THE CALIFORNIA OIL WAR
LONE STAR AND THE ALASKAN GUNS
LONE STAR AND THE WHITE RIVER CURSE
LONE STAR AND THE TOMBSTONE GAMBLE
LONE STAR AND THE TIMBERLAND TERROR
LONE STAR IN THE CHEROKEE STRIP
LONE STAR AND THE OREGON RAIL SABOTAGE
LONE STAR AND THE MISSION WAR
LONE STAR AND THE GUNPOWDER CURE
LONE STAR AND THE LAND BARONS
LONE STAR AND THE GULF PIRATES
LONE STAR AND THE INDIAN REBELLION
LONE STAR AND THE NEVADA MUSTANGS
LONE STAR AND THE CON MAN'S RANSOM
LONE STAR AND THE STAGE COACH WAR
LONE STAR AND THE TWO GUN KID
LONE STAR AND THE SIERRA SWINDLERS
LONE STAR IN THE BIG HORN MOUNTAINS
LONE STAR AND THE DEATH TRAIN
LONE STAR AND THE RUSTLER'S AMBUSH
LONE STAR AND THE TONG'S REVENGE
LONE STAR AND THE OUTLAW POSSE
LONE STAR AND THE SKY WARRIORS
LONE STAR IN A RANGE WAR
LONE STAR AND THE PHANTOM GUNMEN
LONE STAR AND THE MONTANA LAND GRAB
LONE STAR AND THE JAMES GANG'S LOOT
LONE STAR AND THE MASTER OF DEATH
LONE STAR AND THE CHEYENNE TRACKDOWN
LONE STAR AND THE LOST GOLD MINE
LONE STAR AND THE COMANCHEROS
LONE STAR AND HICKOK'S GHOST
LONE STAR AND THE DEADLY STRANGER
LONE STAR AND THE SILVER BANDITS
LONE STAR AND THE NEVADA BLOODBATH
LONE STAR IN THE BIG THICKET
LONE STAR AND THE SUICIDE SPREAD
LONE STAR AND THE TEXAS RANGERS
LONE STAR AND THE DEATH MERCHANTS
LONE STAR AND THE COMSTOCK CROSS FIRE
LONE STAR AND THE MEDICINE LODGE SHOOT-OUT
LONE STAR AND THE BARBARY KILLERS

WESLEY ELLIS

LONE STAR AND THE ROGUE GRIZZLIES

JOVE BOOKS, NEW YORK

LONE STAR AND THE ROGUE GRIZZLIES

A Jove book/published by arrangement with
the author

PRINTING HISTORY
Jove edition/May 1989

For information address: The Berkley Publishing Group,
200 Madison Avenue, New York, New York 10016.

ISBN: 0-515-10016-1

Jove books are published by The Berkley Publishing Group,
200 Madison Avenue, New York, New York 10016.

PRINTED IN THE UNITED STATES OF AMERICA

10 9 8 7 6 5 4 3 2 1

Chapter 1

The air was thin, cool and invigorating. The pine forests surrounding a great Rocky Mountain basin below were magnificent as the stagecoach bounced along the crest of the Continental Divide. It was summertime, and both Jessie Starbuck and her samurai were happy to be where the weather was so fine. Down in Texas, at the great Circle Star Ranch which Jessie owned, the temperature was probably hovering around one hundred degrees. Her foreman, Ed Wright, would be using the cowboys and their horses with care to avoid heat exhaustion. But up here, well, it seemed like paradise.

Jessie closed her green eyes and breathed in the scent of pines. When she opened her eyes again, she could see snow that never melted on the highest peaks and a sky that was the bluest blue imaginable. Mountain meadows criss-crossed each other gaily, and the sun made them sparkle like silver ribbons.

"Ki," Jessie said, stretching her long legs and looking at the samurai who was content to be silent for long stretches, "I like this high mountain country. I'm sorry that my father's old friend, Ned Cotton, is in financial trouble. I'll try to make him take a non-interest loan, but if he really wants to sell his ranch, then I'll buy."

"It's a long way from Circle Star."

"Colorado is good country," she told him.

"I thought you liked rolling hills and grasslands."

"Well, I do, but I also like mountain valleys. There are none prettier in the world than these."

"That's as good a reason as any to buy," the samurai said.

"I've got some even better, if you'd care to hear them."

The samurai, who had also been looking out his window, now turned to her. He was tall and rather slight in appearance. Son of an American seaman and a Japanese woman of royal blood, he possessed fine features and good looks. His eyes were large and dark, and very penetrating. He rarely laughed but never lost his temper. He was dressed in black, and a woven leather band held his shoulder-length hair neatly in place. Instead of boots, he preferred soft leather sandals. Within the secret pockets of his tunic, Jessie knew there were weapons far more silent and deadly than a gun. Ki was Jessie's bodyguard as well as her friend. He was always prepared to give his own life to save hers. That was the way of a true samurai.

"Of course I'd like to hear them, but what I can't understand is why you'd want to own a ranch so far from Texas and your own herds?"

"Well, just look out there. What do you see?"

"Beauty."

"What else?"

The samurai did not need to look again. He suspected that he knew where Jessie's line of reasoning was going. It was not in the direction of what he saw, but what he did *not* see. He divined her method, and it would have been a little deflating to tell her so. It was Ki's observation that most Americans enjoyed the belief that their thoughts, motives and desires were inscrutable. Ki decided it wisest to display ignorance. "I see an eagle on the wing with a rabbit in its talons. They are bound for the high peaks to feed the eagle's offspring. I see elk and deer—"

"And not a single head of cattle!" Jessie interrupted. "Can you imagine all this good grass going to waste? It should be used and it's not! Why don't we see cattle fattening in this basin? Or even sheep?"

Sometimes Ki enjoyed playing the devil's advocate. "I like it fine without cattle and sheep."

"Of course you do," Jessie said, her green eyes sparkling. "But I'm a rancher. When I see lush grass going to waste, it bothers me. Oh, I know the dangers of overgrazing and all that, but it's obvious to me that this basin would support several ranchers."

"Perhaps," the samurai reasoned, "the winters are too hard."

"Yes," Jessie said. "I have been considering that. But even so, this ought to be a fine summer range. A crew of cowboys could push the herds up here in the spring and drive them back down to either Denver or Pueblo in the fall. Same with flocks of sheep! I tell you, someone is missing the boat here. You could run ten thousand head of cattle and twice as many sheep in this basin. Is Ned Cotton having a problem because he can't see how much opportunity is going to waste up here?"

The samurai nodded his head. Jessica Starbuck was one of the finest ranchers in the country and probably the most successful. Never mind that her father, Alex Starbuck, had left her a global-wide empire of industries ranging from diamond mines in South Africa to factories scattered throughout Europe. Jessie had rapidly increased her holdings by dint of her own talent, dedication and hard work. She was the kind of person that anyone would love to work for. She gave responsibility just as soon as a person demonstrated ability. She paid well and was quick with praise whenever her managers met her high and exacting standards. Standards set by her father before his untimely death, which she had always maintained.

Jessie traveled the world and could speak many languages. She had that rare knack of making people from all stations and walks of life comfortable. Her wit, beauty and fire had captured the hearts of kings and playboy princes, who would have given half their fortunes to possess a woman like Jessie. She had declined their offers, yet still managed to remain their object of desire. And that was not an easy thing to do. But most amazing of all, despite all her sophistication, Jessie's first love was her Circle Star cattle ranch. She would rather be out on a round-up than running a board meeting anytime. Jessie was generous and fun-loving.

"What do you think is the reason we see no livestock?" she asked, obviously perplexed.

"I don't know," the samurai admitted, quite serious now. "If you say it makes good sense to trail herds of cattle or flocks of sheep up here for summer range, then I can't imagine why these huge grasslands are unstocked. Could it be that the grass or the water has some element that—"

"No," she said. "If that were the case, you wouldn't see deer or elk grazing them. The only thing I can think of is that there might have been a range war or perhaps all this land is owned by someone who has tied it up for future years. I am looking forward to talking to Ned and finding out the answers. Something is amiss here. Cattle and sheep prices have been excellent the past few years. It should be easy to make money with this much grass and water."

"Do you remember Mr. Cotton?"

"Not very well," Jessie conceded. "I was very young when he came by Circle Star the last time. I remember he had a big laugh and was quite tall and thin. But that's about all I remember before I was sent east to the finishing school my father thought was so important."

"They did their best, and I don't think all their efforts were in vain," Ki said with a trace of amusement. "In fact, I can think of a time or two when you have been in the company of royalty that you actually used the American rules of etiquette that you were taught."

"You've seen him much more recently than I, what is the man like?"

"He is very tall, quite thin and he has a wonderful sense of humor. He had the knack of making your father laugh, and you know that was not always the easiest thing to do. Mr. Cotton is a good man. Your father told me that several years before you were born he was in trouble, and Ned Cotton was one of the few men willing to risk his own life savings to help. Your father never forgot that favor. He would have done anything necessary to help Mr. Cotton."

"Then so will I," Jessie said. "Whatever amount of money he needs to stock these deserted ranges, he shall have at once. And if he needs the finest longhorns Texas has to offer, then we'll deliver them."

"Mr. Cotton is a very proud man," Ki said. "Unless I am mistaken, he won't accept an outright gift."

"I was afraid of that. Well, no matter. If he won't take a loan, then I'll ask him to be my partner. His land, my cattle and cowboys. In a few years, if the cattle prices don't fall apart, we can all make a good return on our investment, and that will solve Mr. Cotton's problem. Besides, it's like I told you, I love the looks of this high country and may just buy a chunk of it."

Ki hid a smile. Jessie loved all country except desert, and though she was remarkable horsewoman, she absolutely refused to ride a camel. She owned sheep and cattle ranches in

Argentina and Australia, New Zealand and Spain. When she traveled, she liked to stay on her ranches whenever possible, learning and accepting the fact that raising livestock was a challenge in any part of the world.

"Junction Station just up ahead. There'll be a half-hour horse trade stop!" the driver shouted. "Good water and bad food!"

Jessie leaned out the window, and sure enough, she saw a stage station looming up ahead at a place where two wagon-roads intersected. Their rutted tracks could be seen trailing off in three new directions. The "station" appeared to be little more than a log cabin and a few broken down corrals. "Funny," she said, "I don't see any replacement team horses."

Ki looked out as well. He possessed remarkable reflexes, and his eyesight was nothing less than extraordinary. Jessie was right, but what she hadn't seen yet were the torn apart corrals, poles scattered everywhere. Usually, at a stage stop like this, the proprietor would have a fire going and hot food ready. But there would be none here because there was no smoke. What Ki saw was two men struggling to control a pack of rambunctious hound dogs. Ki could see that the hounds were all tangled up in their line and giving the two men fits.

Ki ducked his head back into the coach. "Something is amiss here, that's for certain."

They heard the driver swear when they got closer, and it was obvious that he was displeased to discover he would have to drive an exhausted team of horses on down the line, maybe even clear to Denver. He slowed the team to a walk and by the time the stage was within a dozen yards of the station, the shrill yapping of the hounds was loud in their ears.

"What on earth could be going on up there?" Jessie asked with a shake of her head.

"I have a theory," Ki said quietly.

Jessie had been looking at the men and the dogs, but now she turned to look at the samurai. "And it is?"

"Those are hunting hounds," Ki said. "And the corrals have obviously been torn down by a grizzly. You can see the fresh yellow marks where claws have ripped off the bark."

"Grizzly?"

Ki shrugged. "Perhaps that explains the reason why we've seen no livestock in this country."

"But I didn't think grizzly were still roaming in this part of the Rockies. I thought they'd all been hunted out or moved north into Wyoming and Montana Territories. There hasn't been a grizzly killed in Texas in nearly thirty years."

"That may be so," Ki said. "But the claw marks weren't made by wolverine or cougar because neither animal is powerful enough to have torn that corral apart before the horses stampeded in terror."

Jessie had learned a long time ago not to discount anything that the samurai might tell her. He was a man who used his brain before his mouth. Not that Ki didn't sometimes make a mistake, because no one was perfect, not even a samurai. But Ki was generally right on the mark, and his logic was quite exceptional. Jessie had no doubt that he had reached a valid conclusion.

Ki's theory was borne out a few minutes later when the driver shouted, "Where the hell is my replacement team!"

"Grizzlies run 'em off!" the station tender shouted. "And they run me off too 'cause I'm getting the hell outa here on that stage!"

"Who's the fella with them damn dogs!" the driver hollered as the stage rolled to a standstill in front of the log cabin. They all saw the claw marks on the door, which made Jessie's hair prickle. Why, could it be that . . .

"My name," a big pot-bellied man in his sixties yelled as he struggled to contain the half-dozen hounds thrashing around in his tie line, "is Billy 'Tall Dog' Walters! And I am the meanest, toughest big game hunter that ever set foot in Colorado! Why, I been a huntin' the great animals of this world since I was knee-high to a piss-ant. I shot elephants in Africa, rhinoceros in the Congo and tigers in India. I have hunted all the great carnivores of the world, including the legendary Ice Man of the Himalayas and Timbucktoo. I wrestled bare-handed with polar bears and won. I kin turn a catamount into a kitten and . . ."

Jessie didn't get to hear what else old Billy 'Tall Dog' Walters could do because his hounds were raising such a fuss they wrapped themselves up around his ankles and sent him crashing to the dirt. And once down, the hounds piled on their master with yips of excitement, licking his face and slobbering the man half to death. If it hadn't been for the station tender cutting the line and freeing the hounds, old Tall Dog might never have managed to get back on his feet. As it was, Jessie had to hide a smile as the old fool staggered erect, wiping dog slick from his face and looking like three kinds of fool.

Jessie and Ki unloaded from the coach while both the stationmaster and the big game hunter explained their sorry state of affairs.

"The grizzly come again," Walters said. "They come before me and the hounds could get here and kill 'em."

"Kill 'em hell!" the station tender swore. "You and them moth-eaten hounds couldn't kill fleas! Why, if you'd have been one day earlier, them rogue bears would have found and ate you like a kid does chocolate cookies."

The two older men began to square off, and it was obvious that they had no use for each other. The dogs were running around and around the yard, then suddenly, the leader stopped, threw back his head and bayed, the sound of it carrying for miles. Instantly, all six hounds took off on the trail of the grizzly with Tall Dog galloping along after them in their wake as he shouted for them to come back.

The entire affair would have been ludicrous if it hadn't been for those terible claw marks on the corral poles and the station door, and the gruesome trail of blood that they now could see leading across the grass into the forest a half mile away.

"As long as those barking, baying hounds are gone, why don't you tell us exactly what happened?" Jessie said to the station tender. Anyone could see that terror was riding him hard just beneath the surface. "Go on and tell it all," she urged.

The station tender slumped with defeat and toed the dirt as he mumbled, "Well, this whole country has been plagued by grizzly the last few years. It seems that one of them was shot in the rear paw with a buffalo rifle. The bullet blew off the animal's hind foot. There used to be a few Ute Indians lived up here, and they said that the bear was big medicine. All whites would be punished for what one fool done to the giant grizzly's paw! They said grizzlies would kill whoever stayed in this basin."

"Superstition," Ki said.

"Well that's damned easy for you to say! But you weren't here last night when the grizzlies came and run off the horses. And you didn't have to listen to the screams of a horse being ripped apart before it was eaten out in the forest where its body was dragged!"

Ki turned to look at the hunter who had finally managed to call in his dogs. "He's already lost two of them."

Jessie saw this was true. Walters was tying up four dogs

and calling for two more, but they weren't coming back. They'd followed the trail into the forest and vanished. "We had better get him back here. I don't think he should stay alone."

The station tender shook his head. "Tall Dog ain't no big game hunter. He was the Justice of the Peace for thirty years down in Denver. Hell, the biggest thing he ever shot was a jackrabbit. All he ever done was marry folks and sign stuff, oh, and they made him catch truants and bring 'em back to the schoolhouse. He's just a stupid old fool."

"Then we've got to convince him to come with us until that bear is hunted down and killed."

"It ain't *one* bear, it's a bunch!"

"Now wait a minute," Ki said. "Bears never hunt in packs like wolves."

"No, well around here they do! Or at least, they're part of a family. The way most folks in these parts figure it, they sort of learned from the big, crippled bear that it is a whole lot easier to kill livestock and even men that it is to chase down a deer or elk. So they're bold and afraid of nobody."

"There's not a grizzly in the world that can stand up to a big hunting rifle," Jessie said. "Why aren't there men up here hunting them?"

"Men have tried! Why, there's even a five hundred dollar bounty on the one with the missing paw. I saw him once. He's a monster! I shot at him but missed, and that sonofabitch came right at me. I dropped my rifle and headed for the station runnin' for my life. Just made it too! The bear, he took a horse and run the others off. There's been hunters gone after 'em and never came back. They've cleared the range of cattle and sheep, and I guess most of the ranchers are callin' it quits. Hell, from the first snowfall in October until the last one in the spring, you can't move around good up here. Bears sleep but nobody's going to be looking for them because the damned wolves are out in packs, just a runnin' down things."

"How far away is Ned Cotton's ranch?" Jessie asked.

"About eight miles down the line near the end of this valley. Old Ned is tough, and he don't scare easy but he's leavin' too. Bears killed all of his dogs, and then started on the cattle. He's hunted them moren' anybody, but the last time he went out, his horse fell and broke its leg. Ned had to walk thirty miles out of the wilderness. He says them bears were coming after him like he was beehive full of honey. He don't want to talk much about it, but he's as done with it all as me."

Jessie looked out at Walters. "We've got to make him bring those hounds and come along," she said. "He's not up to this."

"He'll get hisself and them damn flea-bitten mongrels eaten for sure!"

Jessie took a deep breath. "Maybe I'm the one that ought to try and talk some sense into him," she said.

"Be a good idea," the station tender groused. "He came in two days ago. I remembered right away he was that same windy Justice of the Peace that everyone said never did nothin' for his pay but chase truants around town. But he's godamighty stubborn. He won't listen to nothin' or nobody."

"Well," Jessie said. "Maybe with two dogs already gone, he'll see some sense in coming along now. I'll give it a try."

Jessie walked out to the man. "I'm sorry you lost a pair of dogs."

He looked up and managed a smile. "Oh, I don't think I really lost 'em. They'll come back after a while. They're probably right on the bear's trail wonderin' why I ain't coming along behind. Fact is, I need a horse to follow them dogs. A man my age, as good as I am, well, I still need a horse.

'Course, just a few years ago I could have run them down afoot, but no more."

Jessie nodded. She helped lead the four baying hounds back to the station. They sure were loud. A few hours of listening to them would drive nearly anyone crazy.

"These hounds are specially trained for bear huntin'," Walters said. "I bought 'em off an old boy down near Pueblo and he's hunted down lots of grizzly with 'em. Got the world's best noses. They could track a swarm of white bees through a driving snowstorm."

"Is that a fact?"

"It sure is! I paid ten dollars each for 'em, and when I kill that big three-pawed devil, I'll have a fine stake. There's a five hundred dollar bounty on him and a hundred on any other grizzly taken out of these parts."

"It's a dangerous way to make money," Jessie said, "perhaps you ought to—"

Walters pushed out his chest and stood to his full height. "I always have thrived on danger, Miss. I tracked wild animals all over the—"

"I know," Jessie said quickly. "You told me already."

"I did?"

"Yes. Now, why don't you come along with us? There's a ranch just eight miles down the line, and I've a friend living there. He can feed us and put us up for the night. The next morning when the stage leaves, you can ride it on to Denver and leave this bear business alone."

Tall Dog Walters started to protest, then stopped and clamped his mouth shut for a minute before speaking. "You say that your friend is a rancher?"

"That's right."

"Then he probably has fresh horses."

"I think he will. The stage horses are wore out and we can switch."

"Makes sense," Walters said, breaking into a smile. "I think I'll come along after all."

Jessie was immensely relieved. The idea of abandoning this ineffectual old fellow and his mangy hounds was not to her liking.

So they tossed the hounds up on the roof, where they immediately lifted their legs and pissed on the trunks and assorted baggage before they started braying.

The stationmaster was furious with the dogs, and so was the driver. As for old Tall Dog Walters, he looked happy enough until the stage jumped ahead suddenly and two of the hounds fell off the roof and hit the ground, howling in pain. "You mean spirited sonofabitch!" Walters screamed in anger. "You did that on purpose!"

As the stage rolled out and the limping hounds began to follow, all Jessie could hear was the driver's laughter.

Chapter 2

The last few miles to Ned Cotton's place was a trial for Jessie and Ki. With two hounds limping along behind braying and howling at their lofty companions on the roof who howled and brayed back, it was too noisy to talk. Jessie tried to block out the infernal noise and concentrate on what she had learned so far. The idea that an entire mountain basin was being held in a grip of terror by a few rogue grizzly was chilling and probably a throwback to another era. Jessie had known a few old mountain men who remembered the days when they had to go through the wilderness with old flintlock rifles and pray that they did not come across a grizzly face to face. In those early days of exploration, many a good man had fired point blank with an old Kentucky rifle only to discover that it had little or no effect on a charging grizzly bear. Unless, of course, it hit the animal in one of a very few critical and vulnerable areas. But with the invention of metallic cartridges and much larger hunting rifles, it became possible to stop a bear or a buffalo with a single shot. Winchester, for example, had brought out its "Centennial Model '76" and it was a beauty. Jessie had one and it was a .45 caliber using 75 grains of black powder which propelled a 350 grain bullet. With that kind of stopping power and the beauty of a repeating rifle, even a grizzly bear stood little chance against a hunter who knew what he was doing.

Ki leaned over and he must have been reading her mind because he said, "Don't even think about going after those bears, Jessie. If there's hunting to be done, I want to do it."

"With your samurai weapons?"

"Of course."

Jessie frowned. Ki used *shuriken* blades and many other weapons including his bow and arrows against enemies. But killing a man with an arrow was one thing, stopping a rampaging grizzly bear was quite another. Jessie knew the samurai was fearless and more skilled in the art of fighting than any five men. But even a samurai's bow was little match against a grizzly, especially in heavy timber where the monsters could be on top of a hunter within a few seconds.

"Why don't we agree just to let someone else do the bounty hunting?"

"I told you both," Walters said, surprising them by the acuity of his hearing. "I'm going to kill the whole murderin' pack of them grizzly and claim the bounty. After me and my dogs are finished, there won't be any more problem with bears."

Jessie wanted to tell the man that he was too old, too out of shape and too slow to go into the forest after rogue grizzly. But she said nothing because she knew that Tall Dog Walters wouldn't pay any attention to good advice. His mind was made up and there was nothing in the world that would change it. Jessie had met thousands of his kind before. They were well-meaning, a little pathetic and entirely dangerous in life-or-death situations. She hoped that perhaps her father's old friend, Ned Cotton, might be able to talk some sense into the man before he got himself and his dogs slaughtered.

"That must be Mr. Cotton's ranch," Ki said, sticking his

head out of the coach a little so that he could see up ahead.

Jessie looked too. Off in the distance, she could see the ranchhouse, barns, sheds and corrals. The scene was prettier than a picture. A river rolled through Ned's pastures and yard. The house was made of logs, but it was large and substantial looking, even from a great distance. This was no poor spread but quite obviously one that Ned had been working on for many years and pouring all of his profits right back into.

"Does Ned have any children?"

"I think he has a daughter back east at school. He also has a son that was going to school at Harvard. Mr. Cotton wanted to make sure that they both had the best education money could buy. I wouldn't be surprised if your father helped make that possible."

Jessie took a deep breath and expelled it slowly. She studied the ranch with a practiced eye. At the far end of the valley, she saw a rider with a herd of cattle numbering less than a thousand. Could that be old Ned Cotton out protecting the last of his cattle? Jessie rather supposed that to be the case.

The stage rolled into the ranch yard, and the lone rider came galloping in to met them. One look at the man, and Jessie knew it was Ned Cotton. He was still tall and straight, only now, his face was deeply lined, and his hair was white. There were two rifle scabbards attached to his saddle, and Jessie could see that he carried a Winchester '76 in both. Good! At least he was primed for any trouble that might come his direction.

While Jessie and Ki gathered up their belongings inside, the others tumbled out of the coach. The pair of hounds on the roof had to be lifted down by Walters. The dogs were raising such a fuss that no one could hear a thing until Ned Cotton yanked out his six-gun and burned their butts with a few careful shots. The hounds went yipping off across the fields, much to Walters's outrage.

"Why'd you have to go and scare my dogs thata way!" he cried.

Ned Cotton answered with his own question. "Are you actually willin' to admit you own them worthless critters?"

Walters and Ned were about the same size and age, but Ned looked to be in a whole lot better shape. Even so, Walters drew himself with an impressive amount of self-righteous indignation and thundered, "Them's the finest bear dogs God ever made!"

"Bear dogs! Ha! They ain't good enough for coon or possum huntin', let alone bears. You keep them yappy critters quiet, or I'll shut them up forever!"

Walters couldn't believe this reception. "Mister, you've got a lot of gall considerin' that I come to rid this country of grizzly!"

"Damn right I do!" Ned shouted. "And if you go after the grizzly, they'll eat you *and* them dogs."

"That's exactly what I told him," the station tender yelled.

Jessie knew that she had to step into this or fists would be flying in a moment or two. She followed the samurai out of the coach and said, "Take it easy, boys! This is no way to act so just simmer down before you make fools of yourselves."

Ned had not seen Jessie inside the coach but now that she was standing before him, he practically fell off his horse. "Jessica Starbuck!"

Ned dismounted and hurried forward, sweeping off his soiled Stetson. "You are prettier than a painting, and I'll bet your father was proud of you. And Ki! Man, you sure look good to this old hoss! Still shootin' that crazy backward bow?"

"Backward to you but forward to me," Ki said, stepping

forward to shake the old rancher's calloused hand.

Introductions were made all around, except for Tall Dog Walters, who was heading after the last of his hounds.

Ned scratched his head in confusion and wonder. "Who in blazes is that idiot?"

Jessie explained without going into details. It was clear that Ned was not pleased when he said, "There have been three or four like him, though most were a good sight younger. They either found nothing, or they found more trouble than they wanted and left on the quick. One never was found, and we figured he got eaten. But at least they all had rifles and horses. This fella, he ain't got nothing but his own foolishness and those four worthless dogs."

"I know," Jessie said, trying to be diplomatic, "but I think if you insult him, he'll just be all the more determined to hunt those bears. So the best thing you could do would be to humor him a little."

"Sure," Ned told her.

The driver of the coach interrupted. "Ned, my horses are plumb worn out. They won't make the pull over the divide. You got a team that'll work in the traces?"

"Afraid not," the rancher said. "All I got is some old brood mares and broke down saddle horses. Ain't a one left fit to pull a stage or that's ever been in harness."

The stage driver cussed under his breath. "The wagon road between here and Denver is too rough and windy to risk taking green horses anyway. I reckon we have no choice but to spend the night, if that's okay with you."

"Sure," Ned told the man. "You can turn your team out with my herd. They'll all stick together, and I'll be riding nightherd so—"

"If you don't mind," the driver said quickly. "I'd sure feel easier if we put them up in the barn."

"No hay to feed 'em," Ned told the man. "I'm even all out of grain."

"You got a sickle, don't you?"

"Yeah, but—"

"Then I'll go out in the meadow and cut them all the grass they need. I just can't chance losin' company horses tonight."

"I understand." Ned looked first at Jessie and then at Ki. "I guess you've heard my hard luck story already. We've got bear trouble, and it's like none I've ever heard of. Jessie, I'm losing one or two horses or cattle a night when there's no moon to shoot by. Even in the moonlight, I'm still losing livestock. That three-pawed bear, he's the boldest, but the others are going to be just as bad. I'll fend off a raid in one place only to hear another going on someplace else."

"I'll be out there with you tonight," Ki promised. "Maybe we'll get lucky and kill the animal."

"Luck is what it will take. I've had a few shots at him. Not many, but a few. He's smart, and he's at war with anybody and everybody."

"If I kill him, the others will leave?"

"I don't think we can count on that. These bears work in the same area and seem to work together, but that most likely is a false impression. My guess is they're just getting bolder and bolder because they've been so successful in outsmarting everyone whose gone after them, including myself. That's why I'd like to sell out to you, Jessie. I got some damned good cattle left though a whole lot of them are scattered all over this mountain and it's going to be damned hard to round them up."

Jessie looked out at the herd. Even if the number lost doubled the number she could see now, they were still so few they wouldn't even be noticed on her huge Texas ranch. "I can always use good cattle," she replied. "But I'm thinking we can beat this thing and keep you here on this ranch. It's a beautiful place."

"Yeah, I know," he said. "Every time I think about leaving it I feel bad inside. Maybe ten years ago, I'd have fought these grizzlies and won, but I learned the hard way that I'm not the man I used to be. I went after them, and . . . by the time I knew what was going on, they were after me."

"I heard about that," Jessie said, seeing Walters returning with three dogs. Apparently, he had lost another one. "Why don't you let Ki and me see if we can hunt a few bear down? We'd need to use those Winchester rifles you are toting on your horse. What do you say?"

"I can't do that," he told her. "If anything happened to you, Jessie, I'd never forgive myself. Your father was the best friend any man ever had. No, I won't let you go out there."

Ki was pleased. He had not wanted Jessie to go bear hunting either. "I will find the one with three paws and kill him."

"What about him and his dogs?" Ned asked. "How are you going to convince the man that he's not up to the challenge?"

"We'll talk to him again," Jessie said. "If he still doesn't want to listen to reason, my decision would be to tie him and his damn dogs down tight on the roof tomorrow morning and take them to Denver whether or not they want to go."

"I'll go for that part of it," Ned agreed. "The man is crazy."

That evening, Jessie had a long, private talk with Walters, and ended it by saying, "It's not that we don't want you to get that bounty, it's just that you might need to rethink things over. You're already down to three dogs, and that's not enough."

"This is a little thin," Walters admitted. "And I still ain't got a horse or real good rifle. I oughta go to Denver like I'd planned to do and then come back."

Jessie pretended to agree. She could only hope that the man would change his mind about bear hunting once he returned to civilization. "Don't worry about standing watch tonight."

"Oh, I got to do my share."

"It's not necessary. You've had a hard day. You've lost dogs, and well, everyone has been a little hard on you."

"It's the hounds bayin' that gets on folks' nerves," Walters said. "To me, it's near as purty as organ music in church."

"I see. Well, if you think you must stand watch, then do so."

"I will," he said. "A man always likes to do everything he can to help others and to help himself."

The night proved to be a quiet one. They stood their watches in turn, knowing that, if there were trouble, a single shot would bring the others running.

There were no shots in the night. After the long trip up from Texas, even the samurai slept until dawn, except for the time he had spent earlier that evening on watch.

The sun was just peeking over the divide when Ki moved quietly outside. He was still, his mind tranquil despite the danger that lurked somewhere in the surrounding forests. He walked to the edge of the nearby river, and when he knelt down to drink, he heard the very faint baying of the hounds. Turning his head to the west, he immediately saw Tall Dog Walters riding across the far end of the basin with his last three hounds trotting along beside him.

"Wait!" Ki yelled, cupping his hands to his mouth, "Come back here!"

His words echoed across the basin, but Walters reined the stolen horse into the trees and vanished. A moment later, Ned Cotton, Jessie and the others stumbled outside. It was all Ned could do to keep from swearing a blue streak when he discovered that Walters had stolen his horse, saddle, bridle, blanket and one of the Winchester rifles.

"Lost," he said with anger shaking his voice. "All lost."

"We can get them back when he returns," Jessie said, trying to calm the man down a little.

But Ned shook his head. "My bet is that he never comes back."

"Then let's go after him," Ki said.

"No!" Ned lowered his voice, aware that he had shouted. "I'm sorry, Ki. This whole thing has got me about to unravel like a cut hemp rope. But going after that fool is not going to help anybody."

"It might help him," Ki said.

"No it won't. He'll either come back with his tail tucked between his legs or he won't come back at all. I'll bet he don't go a mile before he figures he's showed us he has some sand. Then, he'll come shaggin' back without any dogs and sayin' as how he shot a bear and it got away. He'll reel off a roll of lies to us longer than music out of a player piano."

"I sure hope so," Jessie said, worried about the man despite the fact he had demonstrated he was not only a fool, but a thief as well.

"Jessie," Ned said, "listen to me. I need you and Ki to help me drive the cattle I have left down to Denver where we can load them on the Denver and Rio Grande, which will take them down to Raton. You can send a telegram and have your cowboys waiting for my herd. They're fine stock, and I'll let you have 'em cheap."

"I pay top dollar for top cattle," she told him. "And if your mind is set to leave, I won't even try to change it. But Ned, I want more than your cattle. I want to buy this ranch and as much of this basin as I can."

Ned stared at her. "But why!"

"Because it's good cattle country, and I need a high, summer pasture."

"But you've got more land in Texas than a man like me can even imagine. What do you want this damned mountain country land for?"

"I like it," Jessie said. "I like the looks of the grass. You see, down in Texas, we sometimes have droughts. If I had a place like this to trail my herds to, it might save them one day."

"I never thought of that," Ned told her. "Makes sense, though."

"Sure it does. You've got enough grass and water for ten to fifteen thousand head of cattle."

"Aren't you forgetting about the grizzlies?"

Jessie shrugged. "Grizzlies can be shot, and they can be trapped. If they leave my herds alone, I'll leave them alone."

"But they won't," Ned said stubbornly. "They'll just keep coming after your cattle until it hurts. Until you can see your life going downhill so fast you know it can't stop."

"I still want the ranch and this basin," Jessie said.

"The basin, well, I don't know about it," Ned told her. "But the ranch is promised to a man named Rod Herman. He's a rich lawyer down in Denver. I don't like him much, but he's made me an offer when no one else would."

"Have you signed the final sale papers yet?"

"No, but I signed intent papers and shook hands on the deal. I told him I'd stand by my word to sell and sign any other papers when the money passed hands."

"How many acres have you got under title?"

"Eighty thousand."

"And he's paying you?"

"Fifty cents an acre."

Jessie groaned. "And that probably includes the house, the corrals, barns, water rights, mineral rights, everything. Am I correct?"

"Yes ma'am. It includes the whole shootin' match. Thirty years of my life. But forty thousand dollars is not to be sneezed at in these hard times. I can live out the rest of my life very well on that and still leave my son and daughter a nice inheritance."

"Is that what you really want?"

Ned looked away, and his face was grim and pinched. "No," he said. "I got a wife and two children buried on this land and a lot of fine memories that go with them. I don't want to leave. My son, he's finishin' up his doctor's training, and I know he's gone in debt pretty deep. This money will help him square himself and take care of everything."

Jessie understood. "What if I can talk this Mr. Herman into backing out of the deal? Will you sell this place to me?"

Ned sighed. "I sure would worry about them grizzlies."

"I can take care of them," Jessie said. "Will you sell to me?"

"Yeah."

"Good. Then I'm going to Denver to meet with this lawyer and strike a deal."

"He won't deal with you, Jessie. He wants this ranch pretty bad."

"Why?"

"He says it reminds him of where he was raised back in Kentucky."

"Bosh!" Jessie snorted. "I've been to Kentucky, and there isn't a place there which resembles this. Kentucky has its own hill beauty, but it doesn't have mountains like these. He's feeding you a line, Ned."

Jessie turned to Ki. "I will be leaving on the stage today.

Help Ned with the cattle. I'll come and help as soon as I can."

Ki nodded. He did not look pleased by Jessie's decision to buy this ranch, but he knew better than to argue. Jessie valued his opinion, all the more so because he never gave it unless it was asked. It was Ki's observation that freely offered advice was almost always worthless.

An hour later the stage was rolling out of the ranchyard with Jessie and the station tender inside and the driver on top. No dogs, no Walters, no samurai. Ki stood beside a horse ready to begin the roundup. A few minutes earlier, he had thought he'd heard three rifle shots, but he could not be certain. They had seemed to come from the direction in which Walters had vanished.

Ki had an uneasy feeling about Tall Dog and his hounds. A very, very uneasy feeling. One he hoped had no foundation whatsoever.

Chapter 3

Despite Ned Cotton's prediction, old Tall Dog Walters did not return that afternoon or night. And the next morning, he was still gone when Ki and Ned saddled horses in preparation for the first day of what they knew would be a dangerous and difficult roundup.

"We'll just have to keep an eye peeled for that crazy bastard," Ned said. "Most likely, he got himself lost in the forest and ain't smart enough to ride up to a peak and get his bearings."

But Ki remembered the distant sound of three rifle shots. So distant that even he had not been sure that the sounds were just far away claps of thunder. "Where do you want to start looking for cattle?" he asked.

Ned made a sweeping circle with his gloved hand. "We can start in any direction. What my cows do is wander into the trees when the sun gets hot. Sometimes they get in too deep and get either tangled up or turned around. Those that tangle don't last long before a grizzly finds them."

Ki kept looking in the direction that he had last seen Walters disappear. "If it's all the same to you, I'll go off that way and start searching the forest."

"Sure. You may even find Walters—or what's left of him. Just don't go too deep into the forest. It's so thick that if a grizzly charges, he's on top of you before you can even get away. I sure wish that I had that other rifle to loan you."

"I wouldn't use it anyway," Ki said. "A samurai uses the weapons he knows best. The old, tried and true weapons his ancestors have always used to defend themselves and those they are sworn to protect."

Ki followed the man's eyes to his bow, and he saw the tolerant look of amusement flavored with a mixture of real concern. Ki wanted to ease the rancher's mind. "I know you don't believe that this weapon can stop a grizzly, but it has the power to send an arrow straight through the animal's body. I can fire it as accurately as you can a bullet."

"I believe that," Ned told him, suddenly very serious. "It's just that there is no way you can shoot arrows as fast as I can lever and unload bullets. A rifle is better in the brush than a bow that size."

Ki did not intend to argue with the old rancher or tell him about the art of *inagashi*, in which an archer can sustain a rapid rate of fire for as many as fifteen arrows, as fast as a rifleman can lever and release bullets. And while Ki was always the first to admit that a rifle did have certain advantages, so did a bow and his specially made arrows. When hunting, the bow's greatest advantage was, of course, its silence. Gunfire would always draw gunfire, but a skilled bowman could slip and move through forest with such stealth that his opponents or quarry never quite knew where the next arrow was coming from.

Ki touched his heels to his horse, and the animal carried him away. When he looked back a few minutes later, Ned Cotton was trotting off to the east in search of his cattle. The samurai studied the ground and noted cattle tracks. After he had ridden almost an hour, he came upon the tracks of a horse and what he was sure were the paw-prints of Tall Dog

Walters's hounds. Ki dismounted and studied the tracks, then he walked into the forest and saw a well-used game train that had obviously also been used by cattle. It seemed to lead northward. The samurai chose a "cleaver" arrow, one specially designed to sever things. The cleaver could slice through a rope or even a thick wooden flag staff held aloft by an enemy. And Ki believed it could also sever the jugular or vital organs of a charging grizzly.

Almost from the moment he started along the trail, his horse began to get nervous. Ki sympathized with its fear and knew the frightened animal smelled grizzly on the bark of the trees and the branches of the thickets. He would have like to have allowed the horse to run for the safety of the open basin but knew that, if a grizzly came close, the horse might sense its presence first. This would give Ki a precious extra second or two that could spell the difference between life and death.

Ki remounted and rode ahead. The thick canopy of pines blocked out the sun, and the air was much cooler than before. His horse snorted with fear and wanted to turn back, but the samurai was firm. His bow was ready, and every fiber of his body was tense and alert to an almost palatable danger that pervaded the dense forest.

Walters's tracks led Ki around a small mountain and ever deeper into the wilderness. The trail descended into a steep ravine, and Ki followed the zig-zagging tracks down to a narrow but deep and swift mountain stream. The samurai dismounted and drank while his horse snorted and refused water because of its great agitation.

Ki found the place where Walters's stolen horse had jumped the stream and continued on. The forest had grown very still, and every time his horse stepped on a branch, the offended wood snapped with more sound than a man could make with his fingers. Ki looked upward at the thick latticework of branches and pine needles. It would be dark in a few hours and he did not want to be caught in this place after sundown. Like his horse, he could smell the heavy scent of the grizzly, and everywhere he looked, he saw the bark of huge trees ripped high above the ground—the territorial mark of the male grizzly.

His horse whirled so suddenly that Ki was almost unseated. The samurai managed to bring the animal under his control and then turned it back around. He saw what was left of a hound, and there were signs everywhere of a struggle. From the marks on the trail, Ki could read how Walters had come upon the dead hound and a grizzly almost at the same instant. He saw three shell casings, and the samurai knew this was where Walters had fired. It had not been the sound of distant thunder which had disturbed him early this morning.

Ki dared not dismount for his horse was almost crazed with terror. He whipped the animal across the haunches and went on, the bow and arrow ready to be used in an instant. Shadows grew deeper, and the samurai pushed his reluctant mount to go faster. He was sure now that he would find Walters and the hounds somewhere just up ahead.

He did. Walters, or what was left of him, had been knocked from his horse, which had broken away and gone rushing headlong into the forest to disappear. The man's dogs had attacked the grizzly, but they were batted and broken to pieces. Their bodies had been partially chewed and scattered. Walters was half buried under pine needles and branches. The stolen Winchester was lying in a stand of heavy thickets.

Ki knew that the Winchester was valuable and that Ned Cotton would want it back. So he dismounted and tried to lead his horse forward, but the animal was wild to run. Ki held onto his reins with one hand and his bow with the other. He was doing all right. His fingers had just touched the rifle when he heard a roar close by and spun around to see a grizzly coming at him. The horse jumped back and the reins were torn from Ki's fingers. He twisted and dropped, landing heavily on his bow. There was no time to use the traditional weapon so he snatched up the Winchester and just did manage to get it pointed at the huge bear. The grizzly went up on its hind legs and roared. Its front feet ready to crush its victim to its massive chest while its dagger-sized fangs tore a man to shreds.

Ki fired point-blank into the raging carnivore's open mouth. The heavy slug sprayed bone and brain from the back of the grizzly's skull, but it still managed to knock the samurai down and land on him, ripping with its terrible claws and burying its long fangs into Ki's left shoulder, just missing the exposed neck.

Ki tasted the bear's fetid breath and felt the smothering animal's weight pressing him down. The samurai knew from experience that small wounds hurt but that very bad ones were so traumatic that a torn part often went numb. Ki's left shoulder *was* numb, but his right hand was just free enough to grab his *tanto* knife. He jerked its long, thin blade from its sheath and buried the weapon in the grizzly's hard belly. He twisted the handle and a flood of warm blood washed over him. Ki used the last of his strength to yank the blade upward until it struck ribs, and then he probed for the monster's heart. The bear's huge jaws suddenly lost their power. The animal quivered in death and then went limp.

The samurai dragged himself out from under the grizzly. He sheathed his knife without even wiping its blade clean. Then he sleeved the gore from his face and tried to stand. It wasn't easy. His legs nearly buckled, but somehow, he pushed himself erect. Ki grabbed the base of a tree and staggered over to retrieve his bow. He studied the grizzly and dimly realized that it had four paws. It was not the famed bear that seemed to be the most vicious of them all. But it was still huge, and he was sure it had also been the one that had killed Tall Dog Walters and his poor hounds.

Ki slipped the bow over his good shoulder and retrieved Ned's Winchester. He placed its butt on the ground between his feet and managed to lever a fresh round into the breech. For now and for a while, his samurai bow would be useless for it took great strength to bend it to the kind of maximum kill effort that would be needed on a grizzly.

Ki looked all around him. This was a place of death. Within his sight, he could see what was left of man and dogs. The bear looked as if it had fallen asleep. It was lying on its torn belly, great paws outstretched. The only thing that hinted at its death was the bright red blood mixed with splinters of bone that formed a lump on the back of its heavy skull.

The samurai turned away and took one step, his head spinning. He took another and then another, but he found he was swaying so badly that it was necessary to use the rifle as a staff. He gripped its barrel and leaned heavily on it for support as he began to make his way slowly out of the forest. If there were other grizzlies within a few miles, they would have heard the fight, and if the wind were coming in their direction, they'd smell the fresh blood and probably come to investigate.

Ki glanced at the fading light. He knew that he was not going to make it out of the forest before nightfall. So be it. He was not an ordinary man but a samurai. He was also *ninja*, trained to fight and survive in darkness. If the great rogue bears came, he would kill at least one more before he died.

But in truth, he hoped they would not come. Sometimes, even for a samurai, it was better to return and fight another day.

• • •

Ned Cotton had heard the shots and came on the run. Being a man who had hunted grizzlies all his life and who had almost been killed by them only a few weeks before, he was sure that Ki had been surprised and mauled to death. It took him almost thirty minutes of wild riding to find where Ki had entered the forest. It took another hour of plunging through a darkening forest to reach the samurai.

"Dammit!" Ned cried, jumping out of the saddle but making sure his horse could not pull away. "I told you this was no place for a man alone!"

Ki was almost ready to faint from the loss of blood. "Get me on the horse and climb up behind so we can get out of here!" he whispered urgently. "I . . . I think they're coming!"

Ned needed no urging. With a strength born of his own fear, he practically threw the samurai onto his horse. Then the animal wheeled, and the old rancher just did manage to get one boot buried in the stirrup as the animal's whirling momentum lifted him up behind the cantle.

Despite carrying double, the horse ran as if it were chased by the very devil. Ki hung onto the saddlehorn knowing that a fall might kill him and that he would have no strength to climb back on the horse. He was trained in mind and body to fight and to ignore both pain and fear, but as the horse raced blindly forward, weaving along the forest trail, Ki *did* know fear. Not for the moment, but at the thought of falling to the earth helpless and unable to fight and having a grizzly come upon him and eating him alive.

Ki did not fall off the horse. The sun was fading when they reached the open basin. Ned let the horse run until it began to crumble in the front, and then he reined the faltering animal to a walk.

"Your shoulder is a mess, Ki. I got some bandages, and

we'll boil some water. I can sew it up with a hair from my horse's tail, but it'll scar and infect."

"There is no choice," Ki whispered. "Use Indian medicine."

"Oh, I will," Ned told him. "There are herbs and things that I've always used on myself. They work, too! You ain't going to die."

Ki nodded weakly. "That, I know. There is too much yet to do."

Ned held the samurai upright. "I guess you found Walters and those hounds?"

Ki nodded.

Ned started to say something else, but then he changed his mind and clamped his jaw shut. He's seen what grizzlies do when they killed a deer. How they buried it or covered it up after eating their fill so that they could come back later and eat some more. It was too horrible to think about when you realized a grizzly would do the same thing with a man.

"We aren't collecting any more cattle in the forests," he said in a small, totally defeated voice. "We're just going to stay at the house and try to protect those I got left until you mend or help arrives. Then we'll take what's left and get the hell outa these mountains."

Ki had not the strength to argue. But he knew one thing for sure—he wasn't leaving until this was finished and the last rogue grizzly was finally dead.

Chapter 4

When Jessie arrived in Denver, she was amazed at the growth and vitality of the city. New stores and homes were springing up everywhere, and the nearby town of Golden was doing its best to eclipse Denver's rapid development. The town itself had been founded as a jumping off place for the hordes of gold seekers that had arrived in 1859. For a short while, "Pike's Peak or Bust" had been a rallying cry that had brought the "fifty-niners" rushing across the country. As soon as those diggings had petered out, more gold and silver discoveries had been found in the nearby mountains. But even after their gold had played out, towns like Cripple Creek and Central City had continued to thrive because it was fine cattle and timber country.

Denver's greatest advantage was its strategic location. It proudly claimed itself the "Gateway to the West" and scoffed at those who maintained that distinctive historic title rightfully belonged to Old Santa Fe. Despite the fact that the Union Pacific had decided to drive its transcontinental rails through the northern town of Cheyenne in Wyoming Territory, Denver had still prospered, in no small way because Denver's town fathers had boldly financed and encouraged the construction of a busy and profitable line north to Cheyenne. Soon afterward, the Denver and Rio Grande railroad had laid rails south.

The Kansas Pacific had also completed its line from the Kansas railhead towns making Denver a virtual hub of commerce and livestock trading.

The moment Jessie arrived in town, she headed straight to the Federal Building to look for her frequent lover, Deputy U.S. Marshal Custis Long. To her dismay she was informed that both Longarm and his boss, U.S. Marshal Billy Vail, were in Austin attending the funeral of an old Ranger acquaintance.

Jessie's next destination was the Plains Hotel where Alex Starbuck had been a regular customer for many years before his assassination. Francois, the hotel's owner, who was a bit foppish to Jessie's way of thinking, wasted no time in seeing that she received the hotel's finest service.

"We're sorry we cannot give you the Alpine Suite," the manager apologized, prancing about in a display of great agitation and frenzy. "It's rented. If we had known you were arriving, we'd have made the necessary arrangements."

"It doesn't matter at all, and you have nothing to apologize for," Jessie told the man as they walked to the room. The manager opened the door, and Jessie swept past him. The room was spacious and well aired; it had chandeliers hanging from the ceiling and a massive oak bed that looked as if it had been carved in Germany. The room's dominant color was a delicate violet and the original art which covered every wall was excellent. Jessie moved to the window and drew the expensive curtains aside to gaze down into the street.

"Will it meet your approval?" Francois asked, his voice anxious as he stroked his little goatee.

"Yes," Jessie told him. "It's lovely. I will need a bath drawn at once."

Francois was very relieved. "Certainly. Anything else? Anything at all? Perhaps something to eat?"

"I am hungry." Jessie knew that Francois thought beef was

the food of barbarians but that was not the reason why she said, "A Texas rancher gets tired of beef, does the chef have any roast pheasant?"

"Oh, but of course! It will be prepared for you at once. And a little champagne?"

"No, just a modest white wine. French. Please select something that you think superb."

Francois beamed. He was the most knowledgeable man on French vintages that Jessie had ever known in America, and he loved to pick his favorite wines and present them to his most distinguished guests like aged treasures. "Very good. Now, the bath."

The hotelman bowed and so did his employee. "If you need anything, please—"

"Actually, I need a little information on a Mr. Rodney Herman. I understand he is a well known attorney. Can you tell me where he is to be found?"

Francois' swarthy face grew dark with anger. He dismissed his assistant and closed the door. "I did not want to speak freely before a subordinate. But . . . this Mr. Herman, he is a very bad sort." Francois waved his little index finger as if he were scolding the man. "He is ruthless and unprincipled. He preys on the young and the innocent. He is a man without honor."

Despite his affectations and delicateness, Jessie liked Francois and trusted his judgement. To Jessie's way of thinking, the French were interesting in that, as individuals, they rarely understood themselves, yet often had remarkably good insights into others.

"You sound very sure of your feelings. And also very strong about them."

Francois gestured with his entire body. "Though few would believe it, the man is a thief and a debaucher!"

"Strong words, Francois. Too strong to use without proof."

The Frenchman wrung his delicate hands. "I know that. And I confess that I have no proof. Only I can see what he has done. If it were not for my poor, fallen cousin, I would kill him and gladly walk up to face the hangman. But if I do that Nicole would never forgive me. She does not even realize that she is under this man's evil spell."

"I see. Is this man a speculator of ranch lands?"

"He will buy anything where there is the chance of making great profit. He owns many properties, or so I have been told. He is rich . . . not like you, Miss Starbuck, but still rich. It is because of his wealth that he has turned my cousin's pretty head."

"Your cousin is in love with the man?"

Francois sadly nodded his head. "It is a great personal tragedy for me. I fear he has her under his diabolical influence. She is young and impressionable. He has much—how should I say it?—much of the preying animal and also much money to turn a girl's head."

"I see," Jessie said. "Would you like me to speak to her?"

Francois' face lit up with hope. "Tell her I will give her an upstairs room of her own . . . free! And if she will only help a little, I will allow her to eat in the dining room as a guest. She does not have to be at the mercy of that swine, Herman."

"I will tell her," Jessie promised.

"Thank you so much for this. I will never forget your kindness. You do this hotel great honor by being our guest, just as your father did before you."

Jessie was touched by the man's obvious sincerity. It was obvious that Francois was nearly beside himself over the current status of his young cousin. "What is this poor girl's name?"

"Miss Nicole Dupree."

"I may need to speak to her about this matter. There is a chance that your cousin and I can help each other."

Francois' face lit up with hope. "Oh, Miss Starbuck, if you would only see fit to help this wilted flower! She is no longer herself. She wears dresses you would find on Parisian street women . . . It is terrible. If she could meet a lady such as yourself, . . . it might change her life back again. She was such a sweet, innocent child."

"I understand, and I will speak to her. But your cousin is no child anymore but instead, a woman. She must be free to choose her own lover, her own way of living."

Francois slumped. "This I know. But she has chosen badly. Is not such a person entitled to one small mistake? Help her if you can!"

Jessie took the Frenchman's arm and gently guided him to the door. "Francois, thank you for warning me about Mr. Herman. I will be very careful when dealing with him. Where may he be found?"

"Over on North Champa Street. He has impressive offices, or so I've been told. He uses them to impress the ignorant and the unwary."

"Well," Jessie said, "I would like to think that I am neither. Thank you, Francois. You have been most helpful."

"My pleasure," the man said as he bowed, grabbed her hand and kissed it fervently. "And thank you for Nicole!"

After the man left, Jessie bathed while her mind considered what the Frenchman had told her. It was not unusual for money to influence and corrupt poor or naive young women, and it was always a tragedy when it happened. If Jessie could help salvage Francois' cousin, she would do so. Mr. Herman sounded as if he was a wretched individual, and Jessie wondered what possible interest this Denver attorney had in Ned Cotton's ranch and that high mountain basin. Well, no matter, in the morning she would buy the man out and then be done with him.

Rod Herman's outer office was impressive. The first thing a visitor saw upon entering was a magnificent solid silver bust of Aristotle, the Greek philosopher, standing on a carved ivory pedestal. The rest of the outer office was equally unusual and expensive but slightly on the garish side with its red velvet drapes and wall-to-wall Persian rugs.

"Can I help you," a young man dressed impeccably in a formal dark suit asked.

"Yes," Jessie told him. "I'd like to meet Mr. Herman."

"Do you have an appointment?" The young man could not stop his eyes from traveling up and down Jessie's body. "An appointment is necessary."

Jessie extended her card. The young man stared at it for a moment, and then his eyes widened. "I've heard of you!"

"Good," Jessie said cooly. "Now, see if Mr. Herman has a few moments to discuss a matter of mutual importance."

The clerk nodded and rushed away. He returned less than two minutes later to say, "Mr. Herman will see you immediately."

Jessie was ushered into a huge office filled with expensive furniture and antiques like a centuries old Cossack sword and a blow-gun from darkest Africa. The walls were covered with the stuffed heads of big game animals, and there was a rifle case that was as large as a closet and filled with expensive big-bore weapons. Stretched out upon the hardwood floor was the most magnificent bearskin rug Jessie had ever seen. A trophy grizzly from the looks of it and one with a tremendously thick coat. It was plain to see that Herman was a hunting enthusiast and a man who took great pride in his marksmanship.

He was younger than Jessie had expected, and he stood well over six foot. He had a massive lantern jaw and dark, expressive eyes. His teeth were perfect. He had the build of an athlete, but when he came around to extend his hand in greeting, he exuded all the warmth of a mating tomcat. "It is an honor. What can I do for you, Miss Starbuck, and what brings you to Denver?"

Jessie did not believe in playing it coy with anyone, trying to pretend that she wanted one thing when she really wanted another. "My father had a very dear friend whom you know, Mr. Ned Cotton. Mr. Cotton has asked me to buy his herds, and he informs me that he has agreed to sell you his ranch at fifty cents an acre."

Herman did not offer her a seat nor did he stand to address her. His lack of manners was very evident when he said, "I don't understand what concern that is of yours."

"The land is worth much more than that, and I'm willing to buy it from you at a price that will assure you a good profit."

The attorney laced his hands behind his head. Each of his big fists carried three rings, most of them loaded with diamonds. "Why?"

"Because I like the Rocky Mountain grass and water."

"There is plenty of grass and water closer to Texas, Miss Starbuck." Herman leaned forward, manicured hands splayed out on his desk, chin jutting out at her. "Why else do you want the ranch?"

"I'd like Ned to stay there until he dies," she said, not batting an eyelash. "It's been his life for many, many years, and I think he wants to stay and be buried there beside his wife and children."

"And you'd let him?"

"Why not?" Jessie took a chair because she felt as if she were a pupil standing up to recite a lesson before her teacher.

"I can make money up there with cattle. Can you?"

Ned reached for a cigar and lit a match with the nail of his thumb. "Finally, you've offered me a reason that makes sense . . . money. I don't buy anything unless I am sure it will show a profit, and you wouldn't be nearly as rich as you are today if you operated otherwise."

"One has to balance profit against many other factors. Things like loyalty, morality and a social conscience. Throughout the centuries, countries that used poorer countries have always fallen. The same is true of businesses and people."

"Nonsense! It's always been the strong that survive. The weak won't inherit the goddamn earth. The strong will and have. I am strong and so are you. So don't give me any of that moralistic crap about social conscience."

"Perhaps you have a good deal to learn about life," Jessie said, her voice cold.

"Perhaps I do," he conceded. "Would you care to be my teacher?"

He grinned lasciviously at her, and Jessie's cheeks burned. "No, I would not," she told him.

Herman was not offended. He sucked on his cigar and grinned. "I like a woman with candor. I like a woman with your looks. Lady, I'll be equally frank and admit I've heard stories about you. Hell, everyone has heard stories about the rich and beautiful Miss Jessica Starbuck. How much money do you really have?"

"That is none of your business. But in truth, I have no idea."

Herman chuckled. "There!" he said, jabbing the cigar at her. "That's what I mean. *Really* rich people don't know how much they're worth. Me, I'm worth about eight hundred thousand dollars. That's big potatoes in this town. But to someone like you, it's nothin'. The difference between us is, that I made my own money, you inherited yours."

"I've nearly doubled my net worth," Jessie snapped. "But I'm not here to talk about how much I own or you own. I just want to make a deal on the Cotton Ranch and any other land in that basin you've gobbled up at a sale price."

"My price is five hundred thousand dollars."

Jessie made herself smile. "That is ridiculous. It would take you a hundred years of sheep raising to make that kind of a profit."

"Yeah, I know." He shrugged. "But that's my price. Take it or leave it. I know you got more money than you know what to do with, so don't try to get me to come down because I won't."

"Mr. Cotton tells me that he hasn't signed the final papers."

Herman's jaw fell and his eyes narrowed. Jessie knew that she had tapped his vulnerableness. "He's signed the letters of intent and that makes the deal legal in Colorado unless he wants to go to court and face a long, long battle that he'll probably lose."

"I believe my lawyers could research the matter and arrive at a different set of conclusions," Jessie said.

Herman shook his head confidently. "I am a damned sharp lawyer, and I've got that property sewed up tighter than an old maid's purse strings. Besides, your lawyers don't know the people I know in this town. If you push this thing, no good will come of it, and you'll lose time and money. I think you had better reconsider your position, Miss Starbuck. Find another valley to buy. Hell, there are thousands of them."

"Not like this one. None that are a part of an old friend's life."

"Are you aware that the basin is plagued by rogue bears?"

Jessie could see that the attorney thought he had caught her by surprise and that he expected she would be shocked or disbelieving. "Yes, I know about them. I believe that they can be run deeper into the wilderness where they'll have to return to hunting their natural prey, or else they'll be shot."

"Others have tried shooting them, and they've failed. More than one has been killed."

Jessie stood up to leave. "I see that you are a hunter," she told him, looking up at all his trophies. "Wasn't that a magnificent polar bear at one time. How tall was he, I wonder."

"Seven foot, two inches, and he weighed over five hundred pounds. I killed him last year in Canada. I let him think he was tracking me, and just when he was sure I was his, I whirled around and shot him three times through the heart."

"Since you consider yourself such a great hunter, why don't you test your skill against the grizzly bears?"

He laughed outright. "Now why would I want to do a dumb thing like that? If they stay or even spread themselves by spilling into a few more valleys, I can buy up the best mountain range in Colorado for a pittance. Hell, those bears are *this* man's best friend!"

Jessie had heard all that she wanted or needed to hear. "I'll be around a day or two if you change your mind. Good day."

"How about you and me, we go to dinner tonight?" he called after her.

Jessie did not even bother to reply. She came in good faith and stated the reasons for wanting to buy the Cotton Ranch. She had not tried to offer lies or in any way trick this man, and in repayment, he'd insulted her with a price that was utterly ridiculous. A price that showed her he wanted the land for other reasons.

Jessie meant to discover those "other reasons" before leaving Denver. Since she had no idea who to talk to first, she guessed she might as well look up Francois' fallen cousin, Nicole. Perhaps she could be convinced to explain what was behind Herman's motives.

Chapter 5

Nicole Dupree had slept very late that morning. Now, as she crawled out of bed and pulled the window shade aside to peek down at the street, she saw that the sun was high and that it was almost noon. Nicole closed the drapes and massaged her temples with her thumbs. She was a tall girl with perfect facial bones and a nice, willowy figure. Her hair was black, and it tumbled to the small of her back. She found a brush and began to work at her hair, giving it two hundred strokes before it shone and almost crackled with static electricity.

She had just turned eighteen years old, the daughter of a French "communard" revolutionary who had been hanged. Two weeks afterward her mother had committed suicide. Within three years, her two older brothers had become political criminals, hunted by those in power. The Dupree family had to disperse and flee for their lives. Nicole had nowhere to hide in France, and so she had fled to England even though she was only thirteen. Exiled and exploited for her youth and beauty, she had soon learned how to fend for herself. She had become the woman-child mistress of a wealthy land baron who had kept her in a small but elegant flat in London. Between his weekly visits, Nicole had worked hard to better herself by learning English as well as reading the classics. Self-taught, she was wise enough to know that she knew a little about much and much about nothing. From her French schooling, she had learned to read, but from her English lord, she had learned that her beauty and her brains were the keys to her success. Her brain would last many years, but Nicole knew that her beauty was fleeting. In twenty years, even if she took good care of herself, she would not even be as desirable as an unprincipled country wench. This was not the case with men. If they became successful, their money kept them desirable to the opposite sex for many, many years.

Nicole was seventeen when she had arrived in Denver. Like many in Europe, she had heard of the great American West and imagined it to be filled with wild Indians and whooping cowboys. Everyone knew that the West was the last frontier. Nicole had arrived in Denver with little money and great fear but also great determination. She had used the Englishman and now she would find a rich American to use as well.

There had been any number of prominent Denverites to choose from, but Nicole was weary of doddering, fussy old men. She wanted a strong man, one who might even marry her someday and thus ensure her the wealth she had always dreamed of achieving. Rodney Herman's name had struck her eye in a newspaper account that announced his purchase of the largest merchantile in Denver. The account happened to mention his age and that he was a very prominent attorney and also a bachelor. This had been all that Nicole had needed to know. Within days, she had arranged a seemingly happenstance meeting. The rest had not been difficult. Rod was fifteen years older than she and very sure of himself. It would never have occurred to him that a young girl from Europe might actually be using him, instead of the other way around.

When Nicole heard the knock on her door, she assumed it was Rodney. He usually dropped by at midmorning, sometimes wanting to make love to her, sometimes to talk about some highly profitable deal or other that he was about to consummate.

Nicole sighed. Rodney Herman was a very passionate and energetic lover, and Nicole was not a woman who enjoyed such strenuous activity before late afternoon. Maybe if she pretended to be gone or asleep he would go away. Nicole continued to brush her hair.

"Miss Dupree?"

Nicole's brow knitted to hear a woman's voice. "Yes?"

"My name is Miss Jessica Starbuck. I would like to speak to you."

Nicole placed the tortoiseshell brush down on her bedside table and drew the tie string on her nightgown. "I am not fully dressed," she said. "What matter of business do you have to discuss with me? Are you from the millinery store?"

"No," Jessie said. "I am from Texas. I want to talk to you about your uncle and about Mr. Herman."

"I have nothing to say about either of them," Nicole said. "Not to a stranger."

Jessie stood in the hallway. "I think you should talk to me. It might be to your advantage."

"Did Francois send you?"

"No."

"Then why are you here?"

"I need to ask you about Mr. Herman."

"Ask Mr. Herman about Mr. Herman."

"Miss Dupree, please open the door. It's important that we talk for a few minutes. It's very important."

Nicole sighed and unlocked the door. If she sent the Texas woman away, her curiosity would plague her for days. It would be far easier to simply hear what this Miss Starbuck had to say and be finished with the matter.

She unlocked her door and was caught by surprise for it was not often that Nicole came face to face with a young woman more beautiful and desirable than herself, but here she was face to face with the loveliest, most lusciously constructed woman she had ever seen. Jessie's reddish blonde hair, hourglass figure and green eyes were stunning. Nicole retreated back into the shadows of her room. Her first reaction was that this woman was going to steal Rod Herman from her grasp and put an end to her scheme of seduction and marriage. "What do you want?"

Jessie forced a reassuring smile. The girl she saw was slender and much too young to be wearing so much facial rouge and makeup. Miss Nicole Dupree stood before her wrapped in a silk gown, her youthful figure half-girl, half-woman. Jessie felt a stab of pity for the girl who was pretty and would perhaps even be beautiful if she did not grow hard from misuse by scoundrels like Rod Herman. How old was Miss Dupree? Jessie guessed sixteen, but she knew that the girl might be a year or two older. At any rate, she was too young to be the kept mistress of a man like Rodney Herman. "I need to talk with you in private," Jessie said. "May I come in?"

Nicole found herself nodding. She glanced around her room, seeing it in disarray and looking a little tawdry in comparison to the creature who stood waiting. "All right."

"I'm going to come right to the point, Miss Dupree. Your uncle is very concerned about you and wishes you to come stay in his hotel. He believes you would be far happier and better off if you did this."

Nicole's mouth twisted with scorn. "If I did not know my uncle better, I would guess you to be his mistress, though you are too pretty to waste your looks on a man like him. But since I suspect my uncle prefers men to women, Miss Starbuck, I don't understand what any of this has to do with you. I don't understand it at all."

"You're not one to pull any punches, are you, Miss Dupree?"

"No. So please get to the point. What does my dear, twittering uncle want now?"

"He wants what is best for you without you being indebted to anyone."

"My uncle wants what is best for himself. When I first came to Denver, he took me in and gave me a room in the basement! The basement where they kept tools. He would not give up a paying room. Did he tell you that?"

"No."

"Well, it's true. So I found myself something better." Nicole smiled and looked around at her room. "Wouldn't you agree?"

Jessie really felt sorry for the girl. She was obviously bitter and trusted no one. "Listen, now that I've said what I promised Francois, I've fulfilled my promise. What I really want to know is why Mr. Rodney Herman wants to buy a cattle ranch up in the mountain basin just southwest of here."

Nicole relaxed. "You mean the one with the rogue grizzly bears?"

"Yes."

Nicole smiled and found a pack of Italian cigarettes on her armoire. She offered one to Jessie who declined. "I think women who smoke look sophisticated. Don't you?"

Jessie did not bat an eyelash when she said, "No."

Nicole lit her cigarette with childish defiance. "You look sophisticated anyway. I am actually a student of sophistication. Do you know why?"

Jessie said nothing. She wanted to better understand this young woman so she let her do the talking.

Nicole continued. "For a woman, beauty and sophistication equal wealth. Think about it. I have. Am I right?"

"I think there is something to what you said, yes."

Nicole expelled a cloud of smoke. "You want to know why Rod is buying that land. I will tell you, for a price."

Jessie was not surprised. She had learned to size people up very quickly, and Nicole was, if nothing else, an opportunist. "How much?"

"Five hundred dollars."

Jessie made a pretense of hesitating. She would have paid ten times that amount to learn the truth. "Very well."

Nicole smiled. "Good. Meet me downstairs for lunch with the money, and I will tell you."

Jessie nodded. "Just one thing. I won't pay you until I hear the reason. If it doesn't make sense, then I won't pay you anything at all."

"How will you know if it 'makes sense'?"

"I just will," Jessie told the young woman as she left the room. "And I will have the money."

When Nicole saw Jessie exit her hotel and disappear down the street, she hurriedly dressed and rushed off to visit Rodney who ushered her into his office and told his male secretary that he did not want to be disturbed under any circumstances.

The young man winked and licked his lips. He watched Nicole's swaying backside and felt himself stiffen with desire the way he had earlier when Jessica Starbuck had entered the office.

The moment the door was closed, Rod pulled Nicole close and began to undress her.

"I need to talk to you first," she insisted. "It's about a woman named Jessica Starbuck."

"She came to see you?"

"Yes." Nicole allowed herself to be lowered to the big

bearskin rug. She knew better than to struggle. He pulled her dress up until it was bunched around her waist. "Rod, can't this wait? I'm supposed to meet her in just a little while."

"All I want is a little while," he panted, staring at the red garters and the black knit stockings he liked her to wear. His hands went to her, and he tore her undergarments away, his hunger for her making his eyes glaze with desire.

Nicole saw that look. It was the same one that other men had when they looked at her just before satisfying their lust. She knew that the talking was over so she spread her legs and watched him climb to his feet and fight his way out of his pants. "Aren't you even going to take off your shoes and socks this time?"

"Hell no," he said, kneeling, then gripping her narrow hips as he slammed his stiff erection into her.

Nicole gasped with pain for he was large and she was still dry. But in a moment, if she could keep from crying out, she knew that she would be slick and the pain would be gone. She dug her fingernails into the bearskin rug to keep from being shoved across the floor. She made herself relax, and she wrapped her long legs around his waist and almost at once felt the dry pain of their union vanish.

"Oh, Frenchie," he grunted. "You are a little love goddess!"

Nicole hugged his bull neck. "Aren't you even a little curious what Miss Starbuck wanted from me?"

"I can guess," he breathed, pistoning in and out of her faster and faster.

Nicole squeezed her eyes shut and let her lean young body go. She had once heard that women did not like being under a rutting man and had often wondered why she was so different because she liked doing this, especially with a man as big and strong as Rod.

Her own breath began to come in short bursts, and she felt her body being hammered and hammering back. She wanted him to come first but as always, she felt herself losing control. Her heels began to drum up and down, and then she was bucking like a wild horse. She buried her face in his neck and cried out in ecstasy, losing herself completely in the frantic act of their lovemaking.

Rod Herman growled deep in his chest. He felt the young woman's release, and it was the signal that triggered his own explosion. He wondered every time he came inside of her why she did not split up the middle. She was so narrow, but she was supple and strong. When his thick root erupted deep inside her womb, she seemed to open even more, and he knew that she wanted his manhood and his spewing seed. All of it and more.

They lay struggling to gain their breath, locked in little body jerks and spasms until he finally rolled off of her and reached for his pants. "I don't know what I'd do without having you once or twice a day," he said. "You're the best I ever had. I mean that, Nicole."

She knew he wanted her to remain on her back for a few minutes while he dressed and looked. "Cigarette?"

He found one of her Italians and lit it for her. "Just don't burn the bearskin," he warned. "You could go up with it."

She smoked as he finished dressing. When she was sure that he did not want her a second time, she sat up cross-legged, the dress badly wrinkled and still all hitched up around her waist. "Miss Starbuck is beautiful, isn't she?"

"I hadn't noticed."

"That's a lie. You noticed. That's why you were extra hard on me just now. Admit it."

He shrugged. "In some ways, you're wise beyond measure, Nicole. I look at you, barely a woman, and then you say something like that and I realize you may be older than me."

"That's not so old. I need an ash tray."

"Then get that sweet little ass of yours covered and come over here and get one," he said, without heat or humor.

Nicole climbed to her feet and got an ash tray.

"Tell me what she wanted," he said.

"You told me you could guess the answer."

"I can. She came to your room to find out why I want Ned Cotton's ranch. Isn't that it?"

"Yes." Nicole was disappointed. She had thought that this information might also be valuable to him. "But I told her I'd tell her later. I wanted to see you first about what to say. She won't believe just any old story."

He grinned. "Tell her the truth. You see, I've got the rights to that land, and she can hire all the lawyers she wants but it won't change a thing. If we go to court, the case could and probably would drag on for twenty years. By then, I'll have the water and it's the water that I want."

"You want me to admit that?"

"She'd find out anyway if she asks around, which I'm sure she is doing right now."

Nicole was suddenly worried. If Miss Starbuck learned the truth on her own, she might not pay five hundred dollars to hear it from her. "Maybe you could say it was something else."

"Naw. Tell her the truth. Now, you better go because I've got a lot of work to do."

Nicole hated to feel as if she was being dismissed. "Is that all I should say?"

"That's all," he told her as he took the cigarette from between her lips, pulled her to her feet and then ushered her to the door. "By the way, how much are you getting from Miss Starbuck for this piece of information?"

Nicole pretended surprise. "Why, what do you mean?"

His voice chilled and his fingers suddenly bit into her arm. "Don't try to trick me. I know you think you can lie to me, but you can't. I read you like a cheap dime novel. How much?"

She blinked back tears of pain. "Two hundred dollars."

He raised his hand to slap her face, then changed his mind because that would leave a mark. So instead, he grabbed her hair and yanked her head back until her neck was bent full. He saw her eyes fill with terror and he held her like that for a minute. "I could pull your lovely head back another inch and your neck would snap. How much is she paying you!"

"Five . . . five hundred," she choked.

"I want it all," he said. "You belong to me, and I feed and take care of you. Everything you got, it comes from me. Understand?"

She somehow managed to indicate she understood. He released her, and she bent over double, tears filling her eyes, heart pounding so loudly it filled her head. He scared her! He was so close to being a killer.

His voice grew gentle. "I'm sorry I did that. But you need to remember who your friends are and aren't. I'm your friend, your sugar daddy. The only one you have or need. You're mine. I own you, Frenchie. And I'll have you when and how I want. Understood?"

She nodded, then felt him turning her around. His breath was on her ear as he whispered. "Five hundred dollars in my hand tomorrow."

She stumbled out of his plush offices. The clerk stared at her with a mixture of pity and lust.

Nicole grabbed a post outside and steadied herself. She was aware that a pair of old men were staring at her. So she raised her chin and sleeved the wetness from her eyes, as wetness leaked from between her legs. Some day, she vowed. Some day she would take Rod Herman's money and leave him nothing for treating her this way. She would humiliate and hurt him as he did her. And she would be *so* glad!

Chapter 6

Jessie was seated and waiting when the young Dupree woman came into the hotel restaurant. She watched Nicole attract the attention of the predominantly male clientele and saw how she swayed her hips a little more than necessary. Jessie could not help but smile and shake her head. This Nicole was quite a flirt, and her character was probably beyond salvation. Still, there was a youthful exuberance and spring to her step that belied her circumstances, and Jessie found herself wanting to help.

"Please sit down."

"Do you have the money?" Nicole asked. "Because if you don't, then—"

"Please sit down," Jessie repeated. "I thought we might have some lunch first and then talk business."

"No," Nicole said, taking a seat and scanning the lunchtime crowd. "Business before pleasure."

Jessie could see that the French woman was intent on doing this her way. "Very well," she said, taking out an envelope with five crisp one hundred dollar bills inside. She opened the envelope for Nicole to see and then placed the envelope under her right elbow. "I'm ready to listen."

"It's the water rights," Nicole said without preamble. "Rod

says they're going to make him a millionaire before he's fifty. He says that Denver needs them."

Jessie was surprised at the girl's candor. She'd already decided that it had to be either the water or mineral rights to the basin that Rodney Herman was after. It was just a matter of finding out which. "Go on."

"There's not much more to tell," Nicole said, remembering an earlier conversation she had had with Rod about the Cotton Ranch and that entire basin. "Rod also believes he can do quite well with sheep and by logging timber. He figures to hold onto the property until Denver is caught in a real dry year. Then he'll form a corporation that would build miles of flues and ditches to bring the water here."

"A very bold and expensive undertaking," Jessie said.

"Rod is bold, and he never uses his own money if he can use someone else's. He'll go public and sell stock." Nicole shrugged her shoulders and eyed the salad that had just been placed before her. "I don't know much about that kind of thing, but Rod is good."

"Does he know you are telling me all this?"

Nicole started to lie, then changed her mind because there was nothing to be gained. "Yes," she said. "He wants the five hundred dollars. Every penny of it."

"I see. And of course, you'll have to turn it over to him."

"Of course."

Jessie slid the envelope across the table. "I'm sorry you couldn't keep it for yourself. Sometimes, a girl needs a stake to get out from something she's caught up in like a web. I can tell you this, Francois wants you back. He said he'd give you a nice room and a chance to earn your keep."

"How generous," Nicole said with sarcasm. "A little allowance that I can earn for cleaning out rooms and working in the kitchen."

"Your uncle is a good man and a successful one," Jessie said. "I think he really would like to help you if you let him. It seems obvious to me that Mr. Herman isn't interested in helping anyone but himself."

"At least you have that much right." Nicole plucked a piece of tomato up from the salad. "Why do you really want that ranch when it has all those horrible grizzly bears on it?"

"I mean to help an old friend," Jessie said. "One that spent his life on that ranch and doesn't want to leave it."

"And the bears? What about them?"

Jessie thought of her samurai. "I have a friend who will either kill them, or chase them farther into the wilderness where they'll be forced to hunt deer, elk and other game instead of just preying on cattle, sheep and horses."

"That's what Rod is intending to do. He wants that three-pawed bear to skin and put on the floor of his office."

"He's already got one that is the largest I've ever seen."

Nicole shrugged, feeling her cheeks warm because Rod kept telling her that they were going to wear the damn rug out if they kept making love on it every day. "He says the three-pawed bear is even bigger."

Jessie gave the girl the envelope with the five hundred dollars. "You could take that and go over to your uncle's hotel and change everything."

"No I couldn't," Nicole said. "You don't know Rod very well. I wouldn't have the pleasure of spending it."

"He'd kill you?"

"I never said that!"

Nicole started to get up and leave, but Jessie caught her arm and said, "Wait. Don't hurry off just yet. I want you to know that I have the means to see that you are taken care of and that no harm would come to you if you decided to leave Mr. Herman."

"I don't believe that," she said. "He has many, many friends and people who owe him favors here in Denver. Francois is one of them, and he doesn't even know it."

"How do you mean?" Jessie asked.

"I mean that there is a mortgage on the hotel and guess who bought it?"

"Rodney Herman."

"That's right. He's a very clever lawyer, Miss Starbuck. He could think of ten ways to see that my uncle defaults."

Jessie looked at the girl in a new light. "I think I'm beginning to understand."

"Don't think I'm martyring myself," Nicole snapped. "Because I'm not. It just so happens that Rodney is the best chance I ever had to get somewhere in this life."

Jessie tapped the envelope on the table. "Fortunes have been made with a smaller stake than you have in your hands. I could help you invest that money, and you might find that, in ten years, you're worth a great deal of money."

"Ten years is too long," she said. "I want—"

"Excuse me, but you must be Miss Jessica Starbuck, and you must be Miss Dupree."

They both looked up to see a young man standing next to their table. He had a small, black leather bag in one hand and his hat in the other. He was about Jessie's age, and there was still a lot of boyishness in his handsome face. "And who must you be?" Nicole said.

He said with obvious pride, "My name is Dr. Michael Cotton."

Jessie extended her hand. "From the looks of that shiny new medical bag you're carrying, I'd guess you were fresh out of medical school. I heard you and your sister were back east."

"I was at Harvard, but my sister got married last week to

one of my best friends. She'll be living in St. Louis. That's what I came to tell Pa. I knew he'd be disappointed that Sally didn't finish her studies. I wrote him, but he never answered. I thought something must be wrong, so as soon as I was finished at school, I came west."

Jessie saw a strong resemblance between father and son. Michael had sandy colored hair and freckles dusted his nose. Like his father he was tall and had a fine pair of wide shoulders. Harvard might have educated him, but it had not erased the traces of his rugged Colorado Rockies upbringing.

"Have you heard about the trouble up on the mountain?" Jessie asked.

"A little." Michael's smiled died. "It just doesn't seem possible that grizzly bears are killing off all my father's herd. I'd guess that the grizzlies have been getting a lot of help from cattle rustlers. I mean to head out as soon as I can borrow a horse."

"Your father has signed some papers and may not have clear title to the ranch any longer," Jessie warned.

Michael's expression reflected both shock and disbelief. "But that's impossible! Why, we've got kin buried on that ranch. It's my father's life. He'd never sell it."

"Yes he would," Nicole said. "He already has."

Michael drew up a chair between them. "How do you know for sure?"

Jessie waited for the girl to answer. When she hesitated, Jessie said, "Because Miss Dupree works for Mr. Herman."

"What she means," Nicole said harshly, "but is too polite to say outright, is that I'm Rod's mistress. Everyone in Denver knows that, and so would you in a few days. It might as well come out right now."

Michael Cotton was caught by surprise and momentarily at a loss for words. Finally, he stammered, "Well, at least you have the guts to say how things are and not try to hide things. I like that in people. It's pretty rare, you know. Especially considering how beautiful you are. I'd have never guessed. I'd have thought you were an actress or a professional dancer or something like that."

"Really?" Nicole's eyes warmed to the man. "You have a nice way of putting things, Michael. And I'm sorry about your father, but it's true. He's finished up there."

"Not if I can help it," the young doctor vowed. "I may have taken the Hippocratic oath to save lives, but I'll not let anyone destroy my father's life by tricking him into selling his ranch."

"You may not have any choice," Jessie said, glancing up to see Rod Herman come strolling into the restaurant. The big man saw them and wheeled in their direction. "Here comes trouble."

Jessie watched the faces of the French girl and the young doctor. Neither of them could completely hide a mixture of loathing and fear.

"Am I too late to join the party?" Herman asked, trying to make a light entrance into the conversation.

Nicole's fingers crushed the envelope, and Herman saw the money. Without a moment's hesitation, he reached out, took it from the girl and shoved it into his inside coat pocket. His smile was as brittle as carved wood.

Michael Cotton was about ten years younger and thirty pounds lighter than Herman, but neither of those statistics caused him to hold in his angry words. "I was meaning to pay you a visit, but this is as good a place as any to tell you that you're not taking my father's ranch over."

"Why don't we discuss this in private?"

"Because," Michael replied, "there's nothing to discuss."

"That's true only in the sense that your father has already

given me the right to claim legal title to his ranch. I have his signature on the papers, and they have been recorded in my office."

Jessie broke into the conversation. "I telegraphed my finest attorney, and he's on his way here right now. He may not know Colorado law the way that you do, but by the time he arrives from San Francisco, he'll know enough of it to give you a run for your money."

"I welcome the challenge," Herman said, not taking his eyes off the young doctor. "I suppose you'd like to open a practice in Denver?'

"I might. Why?"

"Because I could be of enormous help in securing both the support of the business community and the necessary financial backing to establish your practice. In fact, I even own some prime commercial property that would be perfect for your office."

"I'll do fine without your help," Michael said in a tight voice.

Herman shrugged. "As you wish. But you might one day discover that it pays to accept help whenever you can get it."

"I don't want or need your help, and the ranch stays in our hands."

"We'll see." Herman turned his full attention to Nicole. "I think we should talk awhile in private, my dear. Don't you."

Nicole surprised everyone by shaking her head. "I . . . I haven't eaten yet. I'd like to eat first."

"No. I want to talk now!"

"Leave her alone," Michael said, coming to his feet.

"I don't take orders from boys," Herman said, taking Nicole's arm and dragging her to her feet.

Jessie reached for her gun, but Michael's fist whistled upward in a tight arc that exploded on the point of Herman's square jaw. It sent the bigger man backpeddling into another table where a couple of businessmen were dining. The table collapsed spilling glass and silverware all over the floor.

Herman jumped back to his feet. He rubbed his jaw and shrugged out of his coat. "Nice punch, kid. But it wasn't a knockout punch, and that's gonna be your downfall. Now, so we don't both wind up owning this dining room, why don't we step outside into the alley?"

"Don't do it," Nicole warned. "He's—"

"Shut up, damn you!" Herman hissed.

Michael started for the back door to the hotel. Jessie was at his side. "I hope that wasn't your best punch," she said.

"I'm afraid it was," Michael replied. "The man has a jawbone as thick as that of an ass. I already cracked a knuckle on it."

They pushed into the alley, the dining room emptying and following. When the two men squared off, there were no less than fifty people forming a ring around the two fighters. Jessie was worried. It was obvious that Herman was much bigger and stronger, even though Michael was a little taller.

But when Michael raised his fists and lifted onto the balls of his feet, Jessie took hope. The young doctor had the look of an experienced collegiate boxer, a man who knew how to use his fists.

Herman rushed and Michael dodged aside. His fists lashed out so fast they were a blur. One fist crashed against the side of Herman's ear, and the other caught him in the small of the back, just below the kidney area. Jessie and the rest of them heard the attorney grunt with pain and saw him stagger before he turned and managed to straighten.

"So," he panted, "you're a fancy boxer, huh? Well, let's just see how you do toe to toe. Come on and stand up and fight like a man!"

But Michael stayed back. His left snapped out like a whip, and it rocked Herman's head back on his muscled shoulders. But then the attorney waded in with both fists and landed two devastating punches of his own. Michael took them both in the face, and when he reeled backward, Herman booted him in the kneecap. The doctor cried out in pain and collapsed. Herman kicked a boot at his face, but Michael saw it coming and somehow managed to almost dodge the blow. He rolled as Herman tried to stomp him and managed to crawl to his feet. But his knee was hurt, and he could not dance.

"Hit him!" Nicole cried. "Hit him!"

Herman swung around. The back of his hand lashed out and struck Nicole across the mouth. Her lips split, and she was knocked into the crowd.

"Bastard!" someone yelled as the crowd swung to Michael's side. "Whip his ass, doc!"

Michael looked at Nicole's bloodied face and charged furiously. It was a mistake. Herman caught him in a bear-hug and lifted the lighter man completely off the ground. Suddenly, a cry erupted from Michael and he bent in the middle. Jessie knew that Herman had cracked or broken his ribs. She almost pulled her gun and fired it into the sky in a desperate attempt to end the fight.

Nicole screamed and jumped on Herman's back. She was insane with fury. She reached around and raked Herman's face with her fingernails until the powerful man bellowed in pain and dropped the doctor.

Michael just did get back to his feet. When he saw Nicole fighting like a cat, he took heart and waded forward. His fists were not like battering rams but more like rapiers. They cut and probed. Herman's nose was bleeding, then his mouth. He finally managed to throw Nicole off his back, but before he could set himself and charge, Michael's fists were banging into both of his eyes, half-blinding the man.

Herman roared like a wounded lion. He lumbered forward, but his vision was blurred. Michael caught him with two big uppercuts to the heart. The attorney staggered and tried to cover his lower torso. Michael drew back his fist and sent it into Herman's bloody nose. Everyone heard the nose crack. Herman crumpled like a wet newspaper, his face a mask of blood.

Everyone heard the attorney curse and say, "You'll pay for this, both of you!"

Nicole stepped forward. The attorney's coat was being held by one of Herman's friends. Before the man understood what was happening, Nicole had the envelope with her five hundred dollars. "If I'm gonna pay no matter what, I might as well take this," she said, going to stand beside Michael and Jessie.

"We need to get you both to a doctor right now," Jessie said, leading the hurt pair through the ring of spectators.

"I *am* a doctor," Michael grunted, his voice barely audible as he tried to hurry along but could not because of his bad knee and ribs.

"I know that, but you're in no shape to treat either yourself or this girl." Jessie guided them back onto the main street. "I know of a doctor that isn't intimidated by a man as ruthless and powerful as Rodney Herman. I'll take you to him now."

Michael was too hurt to argue, and Nicole was clearly more afraid now that the fight was over than she had been while clinging to Herman's back and raking his face. "He's got men," she whispered. "They'll come looking for us. We have to get out of Denver! God! Why did I do that!"

"Because," Jessie said. "You hated the man. He treated

you like a dog. When he hit you again, something inside said, *enough*! So you fought. I'm proud of you."

"And I'm a dead woman," Nicole groaned, wiping her bloody lips. "He'll have me killed for sure."

Jessie did not have time to argue with the nearly panic-stricken girl. But she knew that a war had been declared back in that alley. A war that seemed to be all to Rodney Herman's advantage. He had the power and the forces to marshal while she had nothing but the knowledge that she was in the right.

Jessie led them over to a small house on LaFayette Street. Dr. Arnold Potter was in his eighties and retired, but Jessie remembered the man had once taken a bullet out of her father after an ambush. Alex Starbuck had always claimed that Dr. Potter was an unheralded genius with a scalpel. And if the man was good with a scalpel, it seemed likely he was good with bandaging busted ribs and cracked knees.

One thing was sure, Michael Cotton was in no shape to go any place for awhile. So if Rodney Herman was going to send out men looking for them, those men would not have far to go. Jessie wondered if the sheriff would help protect them.

She would see the man tomorrow and seek the help of his office. But if her instincts were correct, Herman probably had that man bought along with a whole lot more. How she wished that Ki were here beside her to protect this pair from harm!

Maybe the samurai and the old rancher were finished collecting the stray cattle, and even now were on their way down the mountain. Maybe, but Jessie knew she couldn't depend on that. She had to be ready to fight on her own.

Chapter 7

The samurai stood perfectly still in the heavy forest. His mangled shoulder was free of bandages for he wanted nothing to encumber his movement. He wore the black costume of *ninja* with its hood pulled down over his eyes so that he could only see through slits.

There were grizzlies in these woods, he could sense them everywhere. Ki wanted the leader, the three-pawed bear, but he knew that it was unlikely he would be fortunate enough to come upon this particular animal.

Just ahead a river gushed through a narrow cleft in the rocks. Ki could see a thin slice of sunlight casting over the water. The samurai had no idea where the river came from or where it was going. All he knew was that the cleft in the rocks was wide enough for him to escape through if a grizzly managed to corner him.

With his injured shoulder, Ki realized that he could not draw back his great samurai bow and release an arrow with enough force to stop a charging grizzly. Even holding and aiming a big Winchester was a near impossible task. Therefore, he must fight the grizzly using some other means.

Ki considered his arsenal of samurai weapons. The *shuriken* star blades were deadly when hurled at a man, but they would not stop a grizzly in its tracks. His knife had the same limitations. Around the samurai's narrow waist was his *surushin*, a six foot length of rope with leather covered steel balls hanging at each end. The *surushin* might be used to trip down a man, a horse or even a grizzly. It could also be thrown at the animal's throat, and if the throw was perfect in every way, the *surushin* would strangle any animal.

Yes, Ki thought, I can use the *surushin*. Making that decision, he made sure that it was wrapped very loosely around his waist so that he could pull it free in an instant.

The samurai studied the game trail leading to the water. He knew that the grizzlies often passed along this way because almost every tree was raked and marked by their spoor.

"I will set a trap," Ki whispered to himself as he reached for the long rope he had brought along.

Ki found a young aspen and roped its crown. Next, he used his practiced eye to judge the distance of his rope against the distance to the cleft in the rock through which he could escape if his trap failed or the grizzly he caught was so powerful it could break or bite through the rope. Satisfied, he used his razor-sharp *tanto* blade to cut a notch in an another tree. He tied a second loop in his rope, and then with great difficulty, he bent the tree over and fastened the loop to the notch. With about eight foot of rope still remaining, he formed a ketch loop and placed it squarely in the center of the game trail. With only two feet of rope left for his lead line, he made it by parting the rope into six strands two feet long and tying them together. The last step was to tie his lead line to the ketch loop and then to bury it just under the surface of the powder-dry dirt. This accomplished, Ki played the lead line out to its full length toward the river realizing that he had no margin for error.

The samurai removed his *ninja* hood now that his trap work was completed. He took a *shuriken* blade from inside his costume and waited for a grizzly bear to come upon him. It would not take long.

Overhead, Ki could hear the sound of birds in the higher branches of the pines. Jays screeched raucously. Less than an hour later, they suddenly flew away. The thick, impenetrable forest grew still and ominous.

"Come face *ninja*," the samurai said, loud enough for the approaching bear to hear. "Come face an honorable death."

Ki heard the grizzly growl in reply. With the segmented lead line gripped in his left hand and a *shuriken* blade in his right, the samurai stood poised and collected. He no longer felt any pain in his badly bitten left shoulder. Nor did he experience fear. He wished he was whole so that he could draw his bow and slay the grizzly in a proper fashion, but *shuriken* and his *surushin* rope would have to do. Perhaps later, if he did not kill the grizzly or was not himself killed.

The bear came ambling into sight. When it saw Ki, it froze for an instant, then growled and lifted up onto its hind legs. Ki looked at its paws and felt a pang of disappointment for this was not the three-pawed beast he had hoped for. Yet, it was a mighty creature. Standing well over six feet tall, its hackles stood up to cover the immense hump over its shoulders.

"If you turn away and leave now, we will both live," Ki told the bear who clawed at the sky and seemed to rotate its head. "But if you do not, one of us will soon die."

The grizzly had no fear of Ki. It advanced to within fifteen feet, still squarely in the path of the ketch loop. Ki could smell the great animal. It had specks of red in its eyes, and its fangs and claws were long and sharp. He knew then that the grizzly was going to attack him.

Suddenly, the animal dropped to all four feet and lunged forward. When its front paw landed over the hidden ketch loop, Ki jerked on his lead line and the ketch loop jumped up to settle around the grizzly's thick forearm. The bear hit the end of the rope, and it was yanked off the tree notch. In an instant, the bent aspen snapped upward, and the bear was caught.

The huge animal was jerked off balance and fell hard. Ki heard the aspen crack, but the tree did not separate. The bear was still anchored by its supple fibers. The samurai hurled his *shuriken* blade at the bear's snarling face. The star blade traveled less than a dozen feet and buried itself in the bear's chest.

The grizzly bellowed with outrage. It slapped at the *shuriken*, but the blade was buried too deep. The animal went crazy. It tried to charge, but the aspen continued to hold. The bear's foot was pulled underneath its body, and the animal seemed to roll up into a huge ball of flashing claws and teeth.

The grizzly bit the rope in two, and Ki sent his *surushin* spinning. It caught the bear around the throat just as the huge beast was gathering to pounce on the man. The rope wrapped itself around and around the bear's throat. The animal tried to claw the obstruction free as it advanced on the retreating samurai.

Ki sent one more blade into the body of the animal before he knew that he had to turn and escape a certain death. He turned and dove into the river just as the bear's claws swiped at him. Ki felt his *ninja* costume shred. Then he was propelled by the water toward the cleft in the rocks.

The grizzly would have hooked him out from the water like a giant salmon had it not been for the *surushin* that was strangling the life from its powerful body. The star blades had not penetrated the thick chest bones, but they were a source of great pain.

Ki worked his way through the fissure of rock, which he discovered was almost a hundred feet wide. The rocks narrowed in one place so sharply that he was caught and had to tear his flesh in order to squeeze through. In another place, he had to go underwater in the swift, cold darkness and hold his breath for over two minutes until he was able to come up and push on through the fissure.

A narrow canyon opened before him. The river tumbled down through its center. There was grass enough for a herd of more than a thousand cattle, but Ki saw only about fifty. And there was one other thing he saw, a horseman. Fortunately, the cowboy's back was to the samurai as Ki slipped out of the water and struggled in behind some rocks.

The samurai stretched outright on the warm sand and studied the cattle. How interesting, he thought, that they are branded with a Rocking C. It was Ned Cotton's brand. Maybe, he thought, grizzlies weren't the only predators in this part of the woods.

The samurai decided to wait until the sun went down, and then he would find out if there were more cattle rustlers to attack. He was very happy by this lucky turn of events but saddened at the thought of the brave grizzly now dead of strangulation.

Chapter 8

Ki watched the sun slip behind the canyon walls. He thought about Jessie down in Denver and also about Ned Cotton who would be frantic with worry. The samurai had promised the old cattleman that he would return before dark, but now that promise would have to be broken. It had been a stroke of good fortune for the samurai to find this hidden canyon. To leave it now without further investigation would be giving up a golden opportunity that might not present itself again. Besides, the samurai was sure that the few cattle and the lone cowboy were just a part of a much larger rustling operation.

As dusk fell, the samurai came to his feet. The grizzly's sharp claws had raked his leg, and the black *ninja* costume was torn and glued to his flesh by his own dried blood. The samurai was not pleased with his own physical condition. He was wounded in too many places and that meant his physical capacities were diminished. He would have to be careful.

Ki limped off, following the trail of the cowboy who was driving the Rocking C cows along before him with his Winchester at the ready. Was the man expecting trouble? Perhaps, but it was likely that he was more concerned about rogue grizzly bears than he was about anyone stumbling upon this mountain hideout.

Ki followed the herd for almost two miles, down through

one canyon after another. It was nearly midnight when the cowboy stopped and made a solitary camp. Ki waited until the man ate his supper, and then he moved in closer to watch. The first thing the cowboy did was to build a huge fire and stack plenty of wood around him. Next, he fixed himself a pot of coffee and fried some meat that he produced from a sack tied behind his cantle.

The samurai's stomach growled, and he tried not to think of food as he watched the cowboy wolf his supper down in gulps. Finished with his meal, the cowboy checked his pony's hobbles, then leaned up against the underside of his saddle and stared up at the stars. He rolled a cigarette and smoked it slowly, then rolled another one. When it too was finished, he settled back and closed his eyes.

As soon as the cowboy dozed off, Ki moved in closer to the fire, not wanting to be caught in the darkness by another grizzly bear who might come to investigate. The samurai was chilled and his clothes were damp. He made himself a bed and blanket of pine needles and drifted off to sleep. In the morning, he awoke feeling weak and flushed. The place where the bear had clawed him was angry and infected. Ki knew that there was nothing that could be done, so he waited for the cowboy to break camp and then followed the man and his small herd.

They traveled steadily southwest, ever deeper into the Rockies, and Ki saw that the trail they followed was well used. It told him that there was a strong likelihood that many other cattle rustlers operated in this part of the country and that they were driving their herd toward a common market. That second afternoon, the samurai flushed a rabbit and killed it with a star blade. He butchered the rabbit and fell back almost a mile to build himself a small fire. As soon as the meat was cooked, he devoured the rabbit and immediately felt stronger.

The cowboy's nervous agitation grew as another day passed. Ki began to wonder about the man's behavior. They were probably far away enough from Ned Cotton's ranch so that grizzly bears were no longer a big concern. Perhaps the cattle thief was afraid of Indians, although the Utes, who had inhabited this country, had already been driven from their lands and forced onto reservations in eastern Utah.

On the fourth day, they came to a small town in the mountains. At first glance, it seemed normal enough, but then Ki realized that there were no signs of children on the streets and the only women he saw were obviously prostitutes. Besides a few wooden saloons, a large blacksmith shop, general merchandise store and a two-story hotel, there was nothing but a collection of tents and shacks along with a some enormous stock pens. Ki knew that he had stumbled across an outlaw's camp, one in which men from many states came and went without fear of the law. The samurai was very sure this was a town without a name.

Ki saw perhaps fifty horses tied to the hitching rails outside the saloons. He watched as the cowboy hazed the fifty Rocking C cattle into pens that were filled with other stolen cattle. Ki could not be sure how many men were present, but he would have guessed nearly a hundred.

The samurai was in bad shape. His shoulder throbbed with pain and his new wounds were red and filled with pus. He felt as if his body were on fire, and he had almost no strength left. Ki knew that he had no choice but to go among the outlaws and see if he could find medical help. The trouble was, his wounds and *ninja* costume would attract attention. Ki saw Mexicans as well as a few Indians on the street and wondered if he could pass as one of them. That seemed to be his only

hope. In an outlaw stronghold like this, men did not ask to
many questions. There were many rough-looking sorts tha
would fight to kill at the slightest suggestion of an insult. K
waited until after dark and then crept into town. Despite his
bad shoulder, he was able to roll a barrel up to the rear wall o
the hotel. Then he climbed onto it and was just able to grab a
ridge of wood and pull himself up through an open window
then tumble inside.

"Hey!" a young woman with red hair and a black eye crie
in protest. "You can't come up here without paying George
downstairs first! You ought to see what he'll do if he . . . why
you're bad hurt!"

Ki struggled unsteadily to his feet. "I've been bitten an
clawed by a grizzly bear," he explained. "Is there a docto
around?"

"No. But there are some fellas downstairs who . . ."

"Never mind," Ki said, staggering toward the bed where
he collapsed. "I just need some sleep and a little food."

"Who are you?" the woman asked, glancing nervously toward the door as if she fully expected trouble to come walking
in any minute. "I never saw nobody come here dressed in
black pajamas and barefooted before."

When the samurai did not answer, she added, "You can'
stay in this room. I'll have another man up here any minute
now. You've got to get out of here!"

Ki tried to sit up but failed. His strength was gone.

"I'm going to get help for you," the red-haired woman
said, staring at the dried blood on his pants. "You're in awfu
shape."

"No!" He lowered his voice. "If they find me in this shape
I'm a dead man. I just need a little time is all. Just a day o
two and I'll move on."

She stopped at the door and turned to look at him. "You'r

in more of a fix than you're telling me, aren't you, Chinaman."

"I'm a samurai," he whispered. "And I don't expect you to know what that means, but I am in real trouble. If you bring anyone up here, I'm finished."

The woman locked her door and walked slowly back to stand beside him. "I don't rightly know what to do, mister. I wish you'd have picked some other window besides mine. If you're in trouble with these people and I'm found hiding you, I'll have two black eyes, and maybe they'll knock all my teeth out to boot."

"I just need a day or two to rest," Ki said. "Just . . ."

Suddenly, there was a loud banging at the door. "Milly! What the hell you got this thing locked for!"

The woman's eyes grew round with fear as her eyes darted from the samurai to the door. "I . . . I . . ."

"Tell them you're sick," Ki whispered.

"George, I'm sick."

"If you don't open this goddamn door and let me in, you'll be a lot sicker!"

The woman's hand flew to her mouth. "I'm sorry," she stammered, "but—"

"Hide me under the bed," Ki wheezed, slipping to the floor and trying to drag his feverish body under the bedframe.

"I can't—"

"You gonna open up, Milly, or am I gonna kick this door down and whip you down to a nubbin'!"

Milly helped shove Ki all the way under the bed, and then she raced to the door and unbolted it. "I'm sorry, I really feel bad."

Ki heard the sound of flesh striking flesh and then heard Milly whimper like a hurt animal. The samurai clenched his fists at his sides and willed himself to stay still.

"Get them clothes off, dammit!" the man named George swore. "Before I tear them off."

"Please, George. Can't you leave me alone tonight! I really feel bad."

"Then I'll make you feel a whole lot better," George said.

Ki saw the man's clothes drop and the bed sagged right down to the samurai's chest as George sat and yanked off his boots and pants. A few minutes later, the sagging bed began to bounce up and down, and the samurai tried to blot out the sound of the couple above. It was clear to him that George was punishing Milly with his body and enjoying every minute of the lesson he was dishing out with such brutal enthusiasm the wooden slats just over Ki threatened to break. His hoarse grunts were a sharp contrast to Milly's whimpers. He used the poor woman hard for almost ten minutes, and then the mattress stopped squeaking. The man's feet hit the floor.

"Sick or not, you're still the best lay in this town," George said. "And if you don't start proving it to more of the men, I'm going to strip your hide with a damned bullwhip."

"I'll try to do better," Milly choked. "I swear I will."

George stood up. "I'll be back tomorrow morning for the money, and you better not lock that damned door on me again."

Milly said nothing as the man dressed. But when the door closed behind him, she began to cry softly. Ki wished he could help her, but he could not. If he were found by George or any of Milly's customers, he was as good as dead.

Chapter 9

When Jessie knocked on Dr. Arnold Potter's door, the old man appeared almost at once. He was short and bald on the top but with plenty of silver hair on the sides of his head. He wore bifocals, and his cheeks were pink. His handshake was firm, and his manner was vigorous despite his advanced age. "Miss Starbuck," he exclaimed with delight, "what a pleasant surprise!"

Jessie stepped aside so that he could see Nicole and the injured young doctor. "I'm afraid it's not so pleasant. We need help, Doc."

The old doctor looked past Jessie. In one glance, he saw that both Nicole and Michael Cotton were in pain. "Come in!"

Potter ushered them into his home, his manner at once professional and confident. Over a career of some forty years of practicing medicine on the western frontier, he'd seen everything and was shocked at nothing. Bullet and knife wounds were the easiest to treat, while internal maladies and infections were the worst.

Once, he'd seen almost an entire settlement die of the cholera. In 1832, it had reached epidemic proportions along the Missouri and Mississippi River communities and thousands had died. Another disease that Dr. Potter had seen kill hundreds of settlers was the ague, so commonplace it was often just called "the fever." Its symptoms were always the same, a dangerously high fever rapidly followed by "the shakes" and vomiting.

Physical injuries, the old doctor thought, I can still handle.

Jessie made brief introductions. "This is Miss Nicole Dupree and Mr. Michael Cotton."

"I know very well who they are," the doctor said, leading them into a small examination room where he still attended a few of his long time and devoted patients. "Mike, tell me this, did you finish your medical training?"

"I did."

"Good! You know I never went to any university. I learned everything from my father who learned it from his father. We studied medicine from books, but we really learned our profession by trial and error. Young man, please remove your shirt and let me see those cracked ribs."

Michael glanced at Nicole. "I'd rather you saw to the lady's lips first."

Dr. Potter hid a smile. "Going to try to start out as a gentleman doctor, huh Mike?"

The young man looked embarrassed, so Potter turned his attention to Nicole. "You've been hit very hard. Closed fist or open."

She shook her head. "I don't know."

"Open," Jessie said. "The back of Rod Herman's hand."

Dr. Potter shook his head. "That man is a brute. I've seen you with him before, young woman. I could have warned you that it was a relationship that would come to this sorry end."

Nicole's lips were badly swollen and covered with dried blood, which the doctor quickly removed with some kind of solution and a couple of cotton balls. Nicole stood looking beaten and so forlorn that Jessie felt compelled to try and somehow cheer her up a little. "Doctor Potter, I wish you could have seen her jump on Herman's back and fight! She did herself proud."

"I lost my head," Nicole said with a sigh. "Even now, I can't believe I acted so crazy."

"Crazy?" Mike shook his head. "Hardly. Miss Dupree, you saved me from having my chest crushed. You're the real hero among us."

Nicole blushed and straightened a little. "I may be a hero, but I'm a stupid one. Rod won't forget that I turned on him. The fact that it was in a public place makes things even worse. He's a proud man. He'll try to get even."

"We'll worry about him later," Jessie said. "Right now, we have to get you both fixed up."

"Open your mouth and let me see your front teeth," the doctor ordered. Nicole opened her mouth, and the doctor examined her teeth. "There are a few that are real loose, but you're young and they'll tighten. I have some ointment for your mashed lips. They'll still be as kissable as they ever were to a young man."

Nicole looked down at her feet. "I'm about run out of patience with men . . . and I mean no offence to you Doc, or to you either," she said to Mike. "But me and men are trouble."

"Maybe you've been picking men for all the wrong reasons," the doctor said. "Money is nice, but it won't buy you happiness."

Jessie almost smiled at that because she had been wanting to tell the girl the same thing.

After the doctor gave Nicole a tube of medical ointment, he turned his attentions to Mike, who had taken off his shirt. "Hurt here?" the doctor asked, gently poking a rib.

Mike flinched with pain, giving a silent answer. Potter's hands moved over his rib cage with the skill of a doctor who had done this many times during his long career. Satisfied, he said, "It's my opinion that the four lower ribs are broken, and the pair above them are cracked."

"I was afraid you'd say something like that," Mike said.

Potter reached for his bandages. "I'll wrap them up good. You'll need to take things real slow for a few weeks. It'll take at least a month before you can take a deep breath without it hurting. Let's take a look at that knee. Please remove your pants."

Michael glanced at Nicole and Jessie. "Not in front of them," he said.

Potter had already forgotten about Jessie and Nicole. "Son, if you still have a sense of modesty, you'll soon lose it after being a doctor."

"We'll be in the parlor," Jessie said, taking Nicole's arm and leading her away.

"What are we going to do?" Nicole asked the minute they were alone.

"I've been thinking about that," Jessie said. "Maybe you'd like to have me buy you a train ticket to somewhere far away."

Nicole thought it over, and even though her first impulse was to take the ticket and leave, she realized there was no where she could hide. "To where? I have no family except Francois and no friends except a few here in Denver."

"It's not safe for you to remain in this city," Jessie said.

"What about Mike? Is he safe?"

"Of course not." Jessie sighed. "Mike is going to want to go up to his father's ranch, and I know that busted ribs and a bad knee won't keep him from leaving. Would you consider accompanying him up into the mountains?"

Nicole's dark eyes widened. "You mean up where those killer grizzly bears are?"

"There's no danger for you," Jessie said. "While I'll admit

they are killing livestock, they'll always try to stay in the forest and away from a man with a rifle. Besides there is a samurai up there, and with him around, you will always be safe."

"A what?"

"Never mind for now," Jessie said. "Suffice to say my friend Ki is as brave and skilled a fighter as you will ever meet. I trust him with my life . . . and with yours and Mike's. Don't be afraid of anything when he is near."

Nicole nodded, but she still did not look completely convinced. "I don't know which I'd be most afraid of," she admitted. "Rod or a grizzly."

"Rod is the one that's the more dangerous," Jessie told her. "No animal in the world is as treacherous and as cunning as man. Will you go with Mike up to his father's ranch and stay there until everything is settled?"

Nicole was not excited about the idea, but there seemed so little alternative that she nodded.

"Good!" Jessie said. "If I don't have to worry about you and Mike, then I can concentrate all my energies on figuring out a way to block that sale and stop Rod Herman from gobbling up that ranch."

Jessie touched the girl's arm. "I don't know if you told me everything before Mike and Rod came. If there is something else I should know that might help save Ned Cotton's cattle ranch, I'd like to hear it."

"There isn't," Nicole said. "At least, not that I know of. Rod might have other reasons besides the water rights. I mean, maybe he or someone else found gold or silver up there, but I don't think so. I really believe all he wants is the water and the timber."

"What about the sheriff and his deputies?" Jessie asked. "Will they help me?"

"I don't think so," Nicole replied. "Sheriff Brown is crooked. I know that he has taken money from Rod for special favors. I'm sure his deputies are also taking a little money on the side."

"I was afraid of that. Then we'll just have to do this by ourselves. I have a lawyer due in the day after tomorrow by train. He'll go to the courthouse and see what papers are on file. Maybe Rod has made some oversight."

"Not likely," Nicole said. "He's pretty thorough when it comes to money."

Jessie was convinced the girl was telling her the truth and had told her all she knew. "As soon as the doctor is finished and it gets dark, I want you and Mike to leave for the ranch. I'll have a horse and buggy waiting behind the house, and I'll be there to give you a signal that things are clear."

Nicole had never had anyone risk their own life to save hers. "You're putting your own life in danger. Why?"

"Ned Cotton once helped my father when he was in trouble," Jessie said without elaboration. "I repay my family debts."

"I wish you could come with us."

"So do I," Jessie said. "When you meet Ki, tell him that he is to stay at the ranch and not to worry about me. I'll see you and Mike later. I promise you, as bleak as things look right now, this will all work out for the best."

Jessie left the girl in the parlor and headed back for her hotel. She was packing a hide-out derringer, but from now on, she was going to wear a six-gun on her shapely hip. Rod Herman was like a wounded animal, and it was true that public injury to his immense pride would make him more treacherous than ever. Given that fact coupled with the sober realization that he had the law on his side, Jessie knew that the odds were stacked against her and Ned Cotton.

"The smart thing to do," she told herself, thinking out loud as she walked, "would just be to help Ned, Mike and Nicole resettle far away and let Herman take that basin. But what would happen if I did that? The man would someday be in a position to strangle Denver over its need for additional water."

Jessie shook her head and lapsed into troubled thoughts. The best and perhaps the only thing that she could do was to wait for her attorney to study the legal questions and documents. If the man could find a loophole or critical omission and beat Herman at his own game, that would be the best way to go. But if not . . . well, she could always pay Herman his half million dollars asking price.

"No!" Jessie vowed, clenching her teeth with determination. "I'll be damned if I'll do that!"

Late that night, Jessie walked along the dark backstreets of Denver until she came up behind Dr. Potter's house. Early that evening, she had seen a man loitering in the shadows out front of the house and suspected that he was one of Rod Herman's men. Now, she wondered if the back alley would be unguarded, but she was not hopeful. Nicole herself had said that Rod Herman was not a man to ignore the details and leave things to chance.

Jessie was dressed in a black wig and a cheap dress with a plunging neckline, which she had bought from a "lady of the night" over on Latimer Street. She wore cheap perfume and there was half a bottle of whiskey in her fist. She looked like a half-drunk whore, and when she saw another one of Herman's spies in the shadows of the back alley, she burped loudly and began to sway a little as she walked.

The man did not move until Jessie was almost abreast of him, and she was afraid that she might even have to fake passing out at his feet to get a reaction. But the guard had seen the outline of Jessie's full breasts in the pale moonlight, and his eyes had bulged along with his pants.

"Hey," he called softly. "How about a little pull on that bottle of yours? A lonesome man can get mighty cold out here in the night."

Jessie stopped. Turned a complete circle, her face wearing a confused expression. She blinked and then smiled loosely. "Oh, hello there! Where am I?"

"Denver town in Colorado."

"I know that," Jessie said. "Can you be a little more specific?"

"Sure I can, for a drink."

Jessie moved closer. The man was of medium height and in his forties. She batted her eyelashes at him in the moonlight. "What are you doing out here in the alley?"

"Waitin' for a woman like you to come along," he said.

Jessie laughed. "I'll bet a handsome devil like you has got lots of women."

"Sure I do. But you're here and they're not. And I got a feeling you're drunk and need help with that bottle. Am I right?"

"Maybe," she said, offering him her bottle.

He took it eagerly. "Thanks! You are a damned good looking woman."

Jessie giggled, handing the lonesome spy her bottle. "So I been told already about ten times tonight. You got any money?"

"I ain't got but a dollar. How much you charge for a little stir of your little honey pot in this alley?"

"Five dollars. I need five dollars. Never let a man touch me for less."

The man upended the bottle and drank deep. He wiped his lips with the back of his sleeve and said. "Five dollars is mighty high. I always pay Denver whores like you two dollars, and after I'm finished, they want to pay me back."

Jessie chuckled. "Now, big boy, you wouldn't be pulling my leg, would you?"

He grabbed her roughly around the waist. "What you say we find us a little piece of grass around here and find out?"

Jessie shook her head. She glanced at Dr. Potter's back porch. The agreed upon signal was that she should light a match, extinguish it and then light a second one. That would alert both Michael and Nicole that a horse and buggy would be coming in a few seconds and they should come outside at once.

The man tried to kiss Jessie but she broke free and said, "Hey, fella, slow down a little! You're just like all the others. You're always in a big hurry. I want a smoke first."

"What?"

"You heard me. I forgot the makin's."

"Hell, I got 'em," he said, taking another pull on the bottle before he handed it back to her. He rolled a cigarette for her and one for himself. He found a match and struck it, and he inhaled before extending the flame to Jessie.

She pretended to inhale the acrid smoke, and then she took a drink and managed to drop her cigarette and accidentally step on it. "Damn! Need another."

"Piss on that!" he growled, trying to shove his hands down her neckline. "We can smoke later. Give me another drink, and let's go find us a place to lay down."

"Nope," she said stubbornly. "I want a smoke first!"

"Here, then, smoke mine."

"Want my own," Jessie slurred.

The guard swore under his breath as he rolled a third cigarette and shoved it between Jessie's pouting lips. He started to strike a second match, but Jessie staggered off.

"Hey!" he called. "Where you going now!"

"To find us a place to lay down," she giggled as she approached the corner of what seemed to be a barn filled with hay.

The man rushed after her. He meant to have her and the bottle, quick-like. At the door to the barn, he caught Jessie and tried to push her into the barn and close the door. But Jessie proved stronger than he'd expected and more truculent. "What happened to my cigarette?" she demanded.

"Dammit woman," he groused, striking a second match and lighting her cigarette. "You better be good."

Jessie forced herself to inhale, and then she blew smoke in the guard's face. "Come on inside and find out," she said.

The guard kept his match lit and grinned because there was a thick mat of musty old hay scattered across the wooden floor. "It'll be a little hard, but I reckon a woman like you is used to worse,'" he said.

The match burnt his fingers, and he dropped it and ground it out under his heel. "Can't see a damn thing in here," he complained. "But I ain't interested in looking at you anyway."

Jessie heard his gun and cartridge belt hit the wooden floor, and it didn't take much imagination to guess that he was climbing out of his pants and boots.

"I hope you're shucking out of that dress," he panted. "Speak up, so I don't stick my dong through a knot hole in the floor, honey!"

"Come and get it," she purred as she reversed the bottle of whiskey in her fist so that she was gripping it by the neck. "It's wet and waiting for you."

"Here I come," he breathed. "I'll give you the dollar later!"

The man jumped at her. Only when he struck the floor, Jessie wasn't there. His stiff rod penetrated nothing but a few inches of prickly hay. When he started to shout with anger, the bottle in Jessie's fist came down hard against the side of his head.

The man went limp.

Jessie searched his pockets and found the dollar. It was important to make the guard think that he had been conned and rolled by a clever Denver hooker. Of course, he'd be too smart to tell Rod Herman that he had been unconscious for a few hours.

Jessie hurried back out into the alley. She saw Michael and Nicole climbing into the buggy and rushed up to them.

"Tell your father and Ki that everything is going to be fine down here. And watch out! When Herman finally realizes that you aren't inside Dr. Potter's house, he'll go crazy and likely come up there looking for you."

"We'll be fine," Michael said. "Watch out for yourself."

"All right," Jessie said. "Now get out of here quick. I'll cover your tracks."

As the buggy rolled away, Jessie pulled off her shawl and began to brush the tire marks away.

With luck, it might be three or four days before Herman's guards finally gave up their surveillance and realized that Nicole and Michael had somehow slipped out of Dr. Potter's house and disappeared. Jessie was hopeful that by then she and the San Francisco attorney, Quentin Daily, would have things sewed up tight.

Chapter 10

Rod Herman leaned back in his office chair and stuffed a cigar in his mouth. The three men who stood before him were all in their early thirties and wore well-used sixguns low on their hips. They were hard looking sorts, especially the one in the middle who was hatchet-faced with a hooked nose, mean eyes and a gold tooth. Rod lit his cigar and squinted through blue smoke. "All right, Wes, tell it to me straight and don't leave out anything."

The hatchet-faced gunman rested his thumbs behind his cartridge belt and said, "That Starbuck woman took Nicole and Mike Cotton over to Doc Potter's house. After awhile, the Starbuck woman came out alone and went back to her hotel room alone. That's all there is to say."

"Nicole and Cotton stayed at Potter's house?"

Wes nodded. "I got two men watching the place, one in the front and one in the back. They ain't going nowhere without us knowing about it."

Herman blew a cloud of smoke. "I don't like the way this is going," he said. "I expect the Starbuck woman is waiting for her attorney friend from San Francisco. I want you to watch her, and when that trains rolls into Denver, you find out who her goddamn legal whiz is and then arrange for him to have a little accident. A fatal accident. Use as many men as it takes but do it right, understand?"

"Sure," Wes said, glancing at the two men flanking him. "We can come up with something."

"Don't gun him down," Herman warned. "Chances are, he won't even be packing a gun. If you shoot him in cold blood before witnesses, there's nothing I can do to save you. It's got to be either an accident, or you'll have to get to the man when he's all alone."

"No problem, unless the Starbuck woman is sleeping with him. What about her?"

"I don't want her harmed. She's too rich and famous to mess around with. Besides, there's always a chance she just might pay my asking price for that basin and save me waiting for a profit."

Wes had other thoughts in mind. "I'd sure like to get into her fancy britches. You mind if I try?"

"Hell yes I do!" Herman bristled. "You and the rest of the boys just leave her alone unless I say otherwise. She's beautiful, but she's dangerous. Big money is always dangerous, and she's got more than she knows what to do with."

"What about Nicole?" one of the gunmen asked. "She still your woman?"

"That's right," Herman said. "She might not agree, but before I'm done with her, she'll be begging me to take her back. And do you know what I'm going to do and say to that two-timing bitch when she does?"

The three grinned wolfishly and waited to hear their bosses' answer.

"I'm gonna make her crawl after me right down the main street of Denver, and then I'm going to take her down to a man in Mexico who will sell her to the Apache. Let her earn dog-meat on her back. They'll bang her on the burning sand with cactus spikes jabbing her in that pretty ass."

The three chuckled. "I got to hand it to you," Duke said. "When a woman crosses you, she's made a big goddamn mistake."

"When *anyone* crosses me, they've made a mistake," Herman said, eyes boring through each of his men. "And that's a good thing for everyone to remember."

Duke shifted his feet. "What about Ned Cotton? We could take care of him."

Rod thought about it for a moment, then shook his head. "Not yet. If we can do this thing without spilling any local blood, then that's all for the better. That way, nobody can accuse me of any wrong doing. But if Cotton shows up pumped full of bullet holes, then there'd be a lot of questions asked."

Wes didn't understand that logic and said so. "What do we care? Sheriff Brown would be asking them, and he's in your hip pocket."

"I know, but let's just take care of Miss Starbuck's high-priced San Francisco attorney and then see what happens. If anything happens, keep me posted. I want to know where Nicole, Mike Cotton and Miss Starbuck are at all times. Is that clearly understood?"

The three gunmen nodded and turned on their heels. When they closed the door, Rod Herman ground his cigar in his ashtray and opened his desk drawer. He pulled out a woman's mirror and stared at the ugly latticework of scabs and scratches that Nicole's fingernails had made across his face. He had put a lot of thought to how he was going to get even with Nicole Dupree. After he had decided that death was too quick, he'd come up with the Apache idea. It made him smile to think of how Nicole would die in the Sonoran desert screaming for mercy while the Indians used and abused her. She was nothing but a cheap, doublecrosser. A whore and an opportunist who'd turned on him in a crowd.

But first things first and that meant getting rid of Jessica Starbuck's hot-shot lawyer. Rod imagined him to be some manicured, big-city dandy. Arrogant and totally unable to imagine that he was as good as a dead man the very minute he stepped off the train.

When Quentin Daily stepped off the train in Denver, he looked for Jessica Starbuck and stood on his guard for trouble. His right hand stayed close to a gun, but his left hand held a brief case bulging with Colorado law books. As he looked around, he remembered when he had come through this town five years earlier on a stage, fresh out of law school. Broke but determined to make his mark.

I've come a long way to get to this point, he thought. And indeed, he had. Son of a Pennsylvania coal miner before he'd won a scholarship to Pennsylvania State College. His mother and his father had wept with gratitude to see their oldest son escape the mines, and Quentin had never looked back. He'd come from tough Irish stock and was accustomed to brutally hard work in the mines. He was a few years older and a lot poorer than most of his college classmates, but he had outworked and outstudied them right into another scholarship to law school. After graduation, he had gone west and had not stopped until he had reached San Francisco where he'd set up his own practice on the tough Barbary Coast. He'd promised his mother and father he would send money every month so that his younger brothers and sisters could escape the hard life that had been the lot of his parents. Quentin had kept his promise. He had two younger brothers in college, and a sister was about to start. None of them, however, seemed to want to practice law for a living, and Quentin could not blame them.

On San Francisco's notorious Barbary Coast, he'd gained a reputation as a fighter, both in and out of the courtroom. After several years of prosecuting criminals, he had turned to real estate law and found it satisfying. He had never worked for the Starbuck people before, but he knew they paid well and were highly respected. That was why, when the chance had come to work for Miss Jessica Starbuck herself, he had grabbed the opportunity and left within the hour.

"Mr. Daily?"

Quentin turned to see the woman he had always wanted to meet. She was even more beautiful in person than in her pictures or when seen from a distance. "Miss Starbuck," he said, extending his hand. "It's a pleasure to finally meet you."

Jessie had not been able to remember his face, but now that he was standing before her, she remembered it quite clearly. "I was present one day when you came racing out of a courtroom. A murderer had knocked the bailiff down and had somehow gotten outside the building. You were the only one fast or tough enough to run him down, though it took you almost the entire length of Market Street."

Quentin grinned. "You saw that, huh."

"Yes, I did. Your athletic ability is admirable."

"Oh, it was just the excitement of the moment. I'm thirty-one and feel every bit my age."

Jessie wasn't sure that she agreed. Quentin was tall and lithe as a runner. He did not have the powerful physique of Rod Herman but instead, was built with the smooth muscles of the samurai. He and Ki both moved like sleek mountain cats. "I'm glad you came despite the warning. Even now, we're being watched. Your life may be in serious danger."

Quentin managed to tear his eyes away from Jessie long enough to study the big crowd of train passengers and those that came to greet them. "I remember coming through Denver on my way out from Pennsylvania," he said. "I liked the looks of this town then. I like it still. Those Rocky Mountains are tall, big shouldered and handsome."

Jessie liked that description. It sort of fit the man himself. "Are you weary or would you like a tour of the town? There's not a lot to see outside of the river, the state buildings and the stockyards."

"I'd like to see them anyway," he said, shouldering his bag. "Let's make the county courthouse our first stop. I want to see what papers have been filed on the Cotton Ranch before the offices are closed for the day. Afterward, I'd sort of hoped you might let me take you out to dinner."

"Oh no," she told him. "You're working for me, and that means I pay the expenses. And as for dinner, I have just the place in mind."

The county courthouse was an imposing brick building, but they had no trouble at all finding the court record's clerk, a fat little man with muttonchop whiskers and an officious way about himself that did not sit well with Jessie.

"I am an attorney, and I'd like to see the recorded deeds and all records and conveyances attached to the Cotton Ranch which would be . . ."

"About twenty-five miles southwest of Denver," Jessie said.

The clerk became agitated. "I'm sorry," he snapped, "but that's impossible."

Quentin's smile froze on his lips. "The documents I have requested *have* to be a matter of public record," he said. "That *is* the law in Colorado."

"Don't tell *me* the law."

"Then don't," Quentin warned, "tell me what I ask is impossible. If it's necessary, I'll track down a superior court udge and get a court order. And when he realizes you've obstructed the law, he's going to be very unhappy. I am sure here are other people who are qualified and ready to replace you after you are fired."

The clerk paled. "Well . . ." he stammered, "of course, I ealize that those records are a matter of the public domain, but I'm afraid they are—at present—being used."

"By whom?" Quentin asked.

"I . . . I forgot."

"Would the person using them happen to be Mr. Rodney Herman?"

The clerk was almost frantic. "So what if it is?" he cried.

Quentin's eyes narrowed. "Excuse me," he said. "But the aw also states that public records cannot be removed from the ecord's office for the very obvious reason that they could be altered."

Quentin turned and looked around the empty room. "And since I don't see this Mr. Herman in this room—"

"All right!" the clerk snapped. "I may have been mistaken. 'll have a look around. But I've other things to do besides wait on you."

"I'm sure you do," the San Francisco attorney said. "However, if I do not have those records in front of me within five minutes, I will escort Miss Starbuck out to find a judge. Have made myself abundantly clear?"

The clerk mopped his face of perspiration and nodded. "I'll have them for you," he whispered, totally submissive now.

"Thank you," Quentin said with a broad smile. "I am certain that it all was a simple mistake and that you are normally a very conscientious and capable man. But in the future, I would make very sure that this sort of thing never happens again."

When the man hurried away, Jessie squeezed Quentin's arm. "You really took the wind out of his sails in a hurry. I appreciate how you've obviously been studying Colorado law in preparation for this work."

"There wasn't much else to do on the train except to get into trouble either drinking or gambling, neither of which interest me greatly. Besides, I've always wanted to work for you, never dreaming that I'd be working *with* you. So I mean to give you good service."

Jessie caught a glint in his eyes, and her heart skipped. "I'm sure you will," she said.

"Here is the deeds ledger," the clerk said, dropping a heavy tome on the counter in front of them. "The Cotton Ranch papers are filed under the 'C' section."

"All of them, including the latest ones filed by Mr. Herman?"

The clerk swallowed and broke under Quentin's hard scrutiny. "There may be a few papers that I have yet to file," he added.

"Then I suggest you get them at once!"

The clerk dashed away, and Jessie could see that Quentin was furious as he began to thumb through the pages of the ledger. "Here we go," he said. "The deed of title, the payment of taxes . . . ah ha! Mr. Herman has been at work here."

"What do you mean?"

But at just that moment, the clerk returned with a document. 'This is all that I have," he said. "I hide nothing, and I want that clearly understood."

Quentin did not answer him but studied the document, his brows knitted with concentration. The clerk wanted to remain, but Jessie said, "That will be all the help we need for now. I'm sure that you have many other duties to perform. We have already taken a good deal of your time."

"Yeah," the clerk said, wandering off while Quentin studied the involved document.

When he was finished, Jessie said, "Will it bind the sale if Herman insists on exercising his option to buy?"

"I'm afraid so," Quentin said. "This Herman fellow may be a real scoundrel, but he is also a very competent lawyer. This document is well written. I can't find a single loophole at first reading, though there are some mitigating circumstances that have been treated just recently in a Supreme Court decision."

"What do you suggest?"

"I think we ought to go see Mr. Herman and—"

"That won't be necessary," Rod Herman said, appearing from the hallway. "I imagine you must be the San Francisco attorney that Miss Starbuck has sent for. Too bad you've wasted such a long trip for nothing."

Herman tapped the ledger and the document. "As you can see, in the matter of my intention to buy the Cotton Ranch, this document is legal and very binding. It includes signatures and witnesses. I have paid the man a hundred dollars legal tender in consideration of the option to buy that ranch at fifty cents an acre."

The two attorneys measured each other from an equal height, but Herman was by far the most imposing. And yet, watching them, Jessie knew that Quentin had steel in him to match the Colorado land swindler and that he would not back down even though he seemed, at the moment, beaten.

Quentin forced a thin smile. "Mr. Herman, as you may or may not be aware, options clauses can and have successfully been appealed and broken in court."

"Not in a *Colorado* court, sir. In this state, we believe in honoring a contract."

Quentin's words were clipped when he said, "This contract

is clearly biased in your financial favor. That means it is prejudiced and may be disallowed. The United States Supreme Court, in the recent ruling of Kincade vs Williams, Clinch County, State of Georgia, threw out exactly this kind of option document for the very reason that I have just stated. You can check on it, if you like."

Herman was not pleased. His confident smile was slipping. "I'll check on it, all right. You can be sure of that."

Jessie decided it was her turn to tighten the screws. "As you can imagine, Mr. Herman. I am not adverse to taking this all the way to the Supreme Court if that is what it takes. I have, besides Mr. Daily, a very skillful legal department on both the east and the west coast."

Herman's anger was ready to surface. "You may indeed!" he said in anger. "But know this, Miss Starbuck. I intend to exercise my option in the very near future. And if this thing goes to a federal court, it may take years. By then, I will have succeeded in draining that basin of its timber and water, and your victory—should you win—would be hollow indeed!"

Quentin clenched his jaw muscles so that they ridged, and the two men stood toe to toe glaring into each other's eyes until Jessie stepped between them. "I believe we have other things to do," she said, leading Quentin away.

Herman called after them, "You might as well pay my asking price, Miss Starbuck. I have won!"

"Not yet you haven't," she replied as they headed out the door. "Not by a long shot."

"You'll be sorry for crossing me in this town!" Herman shouted. "Damn sorry!"

Jessie supposed she might be. But she was up to the fight, and from what she'd seen of Quentin Daily, she guessed that he was too.

Chapter 11

essie studied the man across the table from her as he talked. I guess my mother and father are pretty proud of me for aving escaped the coal mines of Pennsylvania," he said. The scholarship changed my life. Not that I consider myself nportant or especially successful. But what I'm doing now *is* nportant, and I'm able to help put my younger brothers and isters through college. That sort of thing is almost unheard of ack in the Pennsylvania coal country where I grew up."

"It's a remarkable story," Jessie said. "You've every reason o be proud of your accomplishments."

"So have you." Quentin poured the rest of their bottle of ine. "When I first heard about your father, I thought no man ould be that big and rich. It wasn't long before I learned ifferently. Then when he died—"

"He was assassinated," Jessie said emphatically. "It's imortant to me that people know the facts. There was a cartel of orld industrialists who had a crazy scheme of controlling the nternational money market and gaining more power than anyne since Julius Caesar and his Roman tribunal. My father ought them right up to the end and succeeded in thwarting eir twisted scheme."

"He started out poor too, didn't he?"

"Yes. He had nothing but an indomitable belief in his ability. He began by renting a very small shop in San Francisco, where he bought and sold imported merchandise from the Far East. As his import business prospered, he bought a leaky old sailing ship to transport more and more goods from Japan and China. He soon added more ships until he owned a large fleet which captured the Oriental trade and then that of Africa and the Middle East."

"But he didn't stop there, did he?" Quentin asked. "I mean, I heard he was a visionary when it came to the maritime industry."

Jessie loved to talk about her late father. "I think you're referring to the fact that he was one of the first men to realize that the wooden-hulled sailing ships were history. He bought a shipyard and began constructing iron-hulled vessels. At first, just for his own needs, then for the needs of the world."

"And railroads."

"Yes," Jessie said. She was impressed by his knowledge. "I see you've done some reading about my father."

"And about you," Quentin said. "I know that when your father died so tragically you were very rich, but since then you've increased your wealth and influence many times over. You haven't simply laid back in the lap of luxury and let your money grow."

"That's true," Jessie conceded. "My father always liked to cite the Biblical parable about the men who were entrusted with a rich man's coins. If you remember, the one that displeased the master buried his coins to be sure that he did not lose them in some endeavor. My father loved that parable. He said it showed that the Lord meant for all of us to use our talents and abilities. And that also means to accept taking risks as well as to work hard and do the best we can with what we have been given. If we do that much, at the end of our lives, we should have no regrets about living life too conservatively. Life is a test, and to be tested you must be willing to face challenges."

"I wouldn't change a thing I've done up to this point," Quentin said. "I've come far, but not as far as you."

"I had some advantages," Jessie admitted. "But it's not fair to hold them against me. I've tried to do the best with what I have been given. I work hard to promote the economies of the world's poorest countries. I can honestly say I've even helped topple cruel and unwise dictators by financing democracy."

"Why are you risking your life here, over this trivial matter of a ranch when—"

"Oh," Jessie exclaimed, "but it isn't at all trivial! This is a matter of principle. Of honor. That means it cannot be trivial. Quentin, I know from what I've heard about you that you have very high legal and moral standards. That you are virtually uncorruptable."

"Who said that?"

"I have many sources that keep me informed. Before I chose you to come here, I had your background thoroughly investigated. I know more about you than you would imagine. I know the names of your brothers and sisters and much about your personal habits. I know you enjoy a cigar after dinner, and that leads me to ask why you haven't asked if I minded if you smoke?"

"I . . . I was afraid you'd think me addicted to tobacco and the less of me for it," he confessed.

"Not at all." Jessie leaned across the table and touched his sleeve. "My father loved a cigar after dinner. And if you promise not to blow the smoke in my face, I won't mind. But I'll tell you a secret."

He smiled with amusement. "Everything you tell me seems like a secret. You are the most wonderfully mysterious woman I've ever met."

"I love the aroma of a certain Persian pipe tobacco that my father used to buy. It is quite rare, but it smells like perfume and smokes beautifully. And it just so happens that I have some with me . . . along with a new briar pipe. Would you care to try it?"

Quentin took the pipe and admired the extraordinary beauty of its wood grain. "It's magnificent," he said.

"The briar is from Ireland. They say they are the best in the world for the briar has lived since St. Patrick drove the snakes out of Ireland during the first century A.D., and that makes it pretty old."

"I've never had anything so beautiful before." Quentin packed the pipe and lit a match. He inhaled deeply and sighed. "It's an unbelievably good blend, Miss Starbuck."

"Jessie. Please, let's not be formal. Anyway, I'm glad you are enjoying it. I own not only the company that crafts the pipe but also the one that harvests and exports the tobacco."

Quentin reached across the table and touched Jessie's arm. "You almost intimidate me with your wealth and your beauty."

"Almost?"

"Yes," he said. "My mother and father were poor, but they taught me that all men and all woman bleed, and cry and even—"

"Even what?"

"Even defecate, Jessie."

She looked straight into his eyes. Then she saw the merriment in his eyes and burst out laughing when she realized he was making a joke and had the audacity to do it perfectly straight-faced.

After that, they left the dining room and headed back to the hotel. The night was lovely with the stars all ablaze. The town was busy, and they could hear the tinkle of saloon and dance hall pianos. "I always loved Denver," Jessie confirmed. "It has such vitality."

"I sense it too," he said. "The very first—"

Suddenly, two drunks slammed through a set of bat-wing doors and collided heavily with Jessie and Quentin. Jessie was knocked from her feet, and Quentin just did manage to keep his balance.

"Goddamn you!" one of the drunks spat. "If you want to walk a woman, do it where you don't get run over by men!"

Quentin helped Jessie to her feet. "Are you all right?"

The only thing wrong with Jessie was that she was mad. "Yes," she gritted.

Both of the drunks were big, barrel-chested men. One of them poked his finger at Jessie and sneered, "Hey, why don't you take a walk with us? We can show you—"

He never finished his sentence; Quentin's fist slammed through his front teeth and sent him crashing back through the swinging saloon doors. The second man roared, grabbed Quentin in a bear hug and drove him off the boardwalk. They landed in the dirt. Then the man slammed Quentin in the face. The attorney managed to roll the drunk off of him and then bashed him hard. Jessie saw the glint of steel in the lamplight.

"Look out!" she cried, reaching for her derringer but knowing it was impossible to get a clean shot without risking Quentin's life. "He's got a knife!"

Quentin managed to get his hands around the man's wrist and to keep himself from being skewered. But just then, the second drunk came charging outside again, a gun in his fist. Jessie stuck out her foot, and the man yelled as he flew headlong off the boardwalk. He struck a water trough so hard it overturned and spilled water into the street.

Jessie pointed her derringer at the man's mud-covered face.

"Move an inch," she warned, "and you're going to eat lead along with mud. You understand me?"

The man nodded.

Jessie turned to watch Quentin as he struggled in the dirt trying to keep the larger man from burying his knife in the attorney's chest. Quentin drove the heel of his boot down the man's shinbone, and the fellow cried out in pain. Quentin smashed him with a hard uppercut and then followed with a straight right hand. Before his opponent could recover his senses, Quentin hit him three times, knocking him back a step with each punch.

When Quentin measured the reeling drunk and smashed his nose in, Jessie knew the fight was over. She grabbed the attorney and said, "Let's get out of here!"

"Hell, no!" Quentin said. "These men knocked you down, insulted you and then attacked me with a knife! I won't be satisfied until I see them behind bars."

"All right," Jessie said realizing that she was talking to a man who was devoted to the rules of justice achieved through a court. "I guess that's as good a way as any to see just what kind of law we have in Denver."

They hauled both men to their feet and shoved them through a large crowd that had gathered. Down the street they marched into the sheriff's office, where they pushed open the door and shoved the two men inside.

"You've got some new business, Sheriff," Quentin said. "These men attacked Miss Starbuck and I. This one even pulled a knife on me. I want them booked and held without bail."

When they entered, the sheriff was sitting at his desk picking his teeth with a knife. He was a sloppy-looking man in his early fifties with mule ears and tobacco-stained teeth. He looked better suited for bib overalls and pig slopping on some poor farm then for law enforcement.

"I'll put them in jail for tonight and let them sober up," the sheriff said, dropping his boots to the floor and dragging himself erect. He stuffed his shirtails around his bulging belly and stifled a yawn. "But I doubt they'll ever get to a court. These boys probably just had a little too much to drink and got rambunctious."

The sheriff's blase attitude infuriated Jessie. "I don't think they're a bit drunk," she stormed. "I think this whole thing was an act staged to provoke and then to kill my attorney. I won't be satisfied with anything less than attempted murder charges."

"Haw!" the sheriff crowed. "Miss, I don't know who you are, but even if you were the damned queen of England, you couldn't get that kind of charge to stick. Why, this is the West! Men get drunk and they fight."

Jessie wanted to grab the sheriff by his dirty shirt-front and shake him like a bag of oats, but she held herself in check.

Now it was Quentin who seemed the more cool-headed. "Jessie, I'm afraid the sheriff has a point. Attempted murder charges would never stick. We can't even prove they're sober, let alone involved in some murder attempt."

"The man is right," the sheriff said. "Most they'll get is a day or two in jail. Besides, no matter what you say, they look drunk as hell to me, and that's just what I'll tell the judge in the morning. You see, the citizens of Denver aren't so all-fired anxious to pay for the upkeep of prisoners. Now, these boys may have started the fight, but from the looks of their faces, they didn't finish it. Beats me how you think a judge is going to go for a charge of attempted murder. Why, you done busted that one poor fella's nose. Look at the mess his face is in! And the other one is all muddied up. They might even press charges against *you*!"

"Let's get out of here," Quentin said. "Before I lose my temper and stuff this hayseed of a sheriff into his own cell."

"Now wait just a minute there!" the sheriff blustered. "You can't talk to an officer of the law like that."

"You're nothing but a buffoon!" Quentin said with heat in his voice.

Jessie sized up the situation and realized that she had better get her hot-tempered Irish attorney out of the sheriff's office before he forgot about the law and bounced the incompetent and obviously corrupt sheriff out on his ear.

She took him by the arm and practically dragged him through the door. "I think you need a drink," she said to him. "A glass of good whiskey."

He was still furious. "I like Denver, but so far, its public servants are the worst I ever came across. Sure, I'd like a drink," he said, lowering his voice. "Have you got any place special in mind?"

"I do," Jessie said. "My hotel room."

Quentin was caught off guard, but he recovered very quickly. "Why, that would be just fine!" he said, taking her arm.

They walked along the boardwalk, and some of the town people who had seen the fight congratulated both Jessie and Quentin for knowing how to handle themselves.

"An attorney, an editor or even a frontier doctor had better know how to fight," Quentin said.

"You say that, despite the fact that you are sworn to live by the law?"

"I see no conflict," he told her. "There is nothing in the law that says an attorney should not concern himself with self-preservation whenever his life or limb is in jeopardy. And there have been more than a few miscarriages of justice that need to be rectified."

"What does that mean?"

Quentin walked along for several minutes, his mind troubled. "There have been a couple of occasions when I took the law into my own hand after it failed to deliver justice," he said quietly. "It's not something I've ever admitted to anyone before, but I have hunted down two murderers who were freed on technicalities in the law."

Jessie stopped on the boardwalk in front of her hotel and looked up at his handsome, but troubled face. "And?"

"And I faced them openly, and I killed them. One with a knife, the other with a gun. I always acted in front of witnesses and let them make the first move. So in both cases, it was ruled self-defense. But I know in my heart I provoked the killings and am morally guilty."

"I don't see it that way," Jessie said. "Not at all. And while I understand that the concept of vigilante justice must seem barbaric to a man learned in the law, it served a vital purpose during the taming of the West. There was often no court or even a sheriff or a jail to take a horse thief, a cattle rustler, murderer or rapist. So they hung him, and then went on with the business of trying to survive."

"I understand that," Quentin said. "But those days are over. We either live by the law, or revert to the rule of might is right. That leaves the weak and the poor without protection."

Jessie agreed. "You're a credit to your profession," she said. "But don't let your conscience stand in the way of what is right and what is wrong. Sometimes, a person has to live by his own law."

"I get a feeling you do that quite often," Quentin said.

"I deal with strong men all over the world," Jessie said. "And in every country, the laws are different and yet somehow very much the same. There are certain things that are always wrong."

They said no more about it. As soon as they were in her room, Jessie locked the door and said, "I am not a woman who normally propositions men that work for me, but you . . . you are impressive and—"

He didn't let her finish, but instead crushed her in his arms. He lifted and carried her to the huge bed with its ornate, hand-carved headboard. "I'm not sure I will be as good a lover as you hope," he told her. "I've never had a woman as desirable as you, and I may be in a rush."

Jessie smiled. "I like you most because you are honest," she said, kissing his mouth. "And I have to admit, from what I've seen so far, when it comes time for action, you are quick with your facts and your fists."

He grinned. "And I may be a little quick the first time we make love."

"The first time? That implies you are pretty certain there'll be a second time."

"There has to be," he whispered, his lips trailing down to the hollow of her throat as his hands began to explore the ways to unbutton her dress.

Jessie helped the man, and when she had slipped out of the last of her garments, Quentin just stared at her body. He could not seem to take his eyes off her long, tapered legs, her narrow waist and full, firm breasts. And when he pulled off his clothes, he was stiff and ready.

Jessie also took a moment to admire Quentin. Besides his large rod, he had a beautiful physique with smooth muscles and a flat, hard belly. "Come on," she said, lying back on the bed and reaching for him.

His lips sought the sensitive buds of her breasts and made them stand as taut as baby roses. Jessie's hand slipped down between their bodies and found his throbbing manhood. "I'm in a hurry too," she panted, stroking his rod and then feeling him lift up above her.

She spread her legs wide and guided his thick shaft down into her dark, golden honey pot. When he entered, she bit her lower lip and sighed with contentment for she was already wet with desire. "Please don't move."

He held himself in rigid control, and she could feel his pulse within her. Beating faster and faster. Before a minute had passed, he was trembling like a leaf. Then she reached down and dug her fingernails into his buttocks and began to move against him. Almost at once, Quentin became a wild thing, bucking and slamming at her until she was caught up in his passion.

But now she was the one in for the surprise because her own body tricked her, and soon she was crying out as wave after wave of powerful spasms rocked her from head to toe.

"Done yet?" he asked, slowing the pace as he looked down into her green eyes.

"You tricked me!" she cried with mock indignation. "In bed, you're not quick at all!"

"No," he said. "But before I'm done, you'll be very glad."

Jessie locked her heels behind his back and began to milk him powerfully. "I think it's your turn to be in for a surprise," she said.

Minutes later, he was losing control, and his moans of pleasure filled the room as he took her with increasingly deep and forceful strokes. Strokes that quickly grew ragged and erratic until he drove into her with one final, frenzied lunge. She felt his hot seed filling her completely.

"If you're as good before a judge and jury as you are in bed," she sighed when their bodies finally grew still, "you'll do just fine."

Quentin Daily kissed her breasts and starting moving on her again. "Jessie," he said. "Before morning, you'll think I'm a raving genius."

Jessie closed her eyes and let her body drink in the sensations he delivered. She did not know what tomorrow might bring, but she was pretty damn sure that tonight was going to be paradise.

Chapter 12

Ned Cotton finished oiling his Winchester, and then he slowly loaded it, thinking about what he was about to do and realizing that he might never again see his ranch, his son or his daughter. He was going after the samurai who had been missing for two days. Missing, Ned thought, and probably dead and already eaten by a grizzly.

Ned ran an oily cleaning rag along the barrel of his rifle, carefully wiping away his finger prints. He had fashioned a sling for the weapon that allowed him to carry it horizontal to the ground at all times. When a grizzly charged out of the forest, there was no time to be wasted yanking a rifle out of a scabbard. Grizzlies were damned hard to stop, and you needed to pump as much lead into them as you could before they got within striking range with their great paws.

Satisfied that the rifle was ready, Ned looped the sling over his left shoulder so that the rifle was under his right arm. Then, he gathered up a sack of dried jerky and extra ammunition and trudged out of his ranch house.

Ned's horse was waiting for him, and the animal seemed to anticipate the danger that lay ahead. It stomped the earth nervously, and its black eyes rolled until the whites seemed unnaturally large.

"Nothin' or nobody lives forever," Ned told the spooked

animal. "Not you, horse, not me, and not Old Three Paws, who probably already ate the samurai."

Ned mounted stiffly and rode off across the long, grassy basin, which, in the past at this time of year, was filled with grazing cattle. It was a fine day, with the sun shining and the birds singing as they flitted across the meadow. Bees were buzzing over the wild flowers, and the sky was as deep a blue as a man would ever see in this world. Yes, Ned thought, it was a day fit for dying.

He followed Ki's cold trail, and when he reached the line of timber, his horse balked. Ned had to use his spurs hard on the animal's flanks in order to get it into the heavy timber. Suddenly, the sun was nearly gone. Under the great canopy of pine boughs, the forest was dim, and there was barely enough light to see the squirrels chattering down at him with defiance and indignation. Wrens flitted through the branches, and two angry blue jays squabbled over their territorial rights.

But Ned appreciated the noise. It meant that there was no immediate danger. He continued on, the Winchester resting easily, a bullet ready at the touch of his finger.

His eyes were not as sharp as they used to be, and because of this, the old cattle rancher was forced to climb on and off his horse many times. Had Ki been riding a horse, the tracking would have been easy. But on foot, the samurai had left little evidence of his silent passage.

The morning passed slowly, and Ned did not hurry either himself or his nervous horse. He moved with deliberate patience, every one of his failing senses working hard to alert him the instant that danger approached. And it *would* approach. He knew that a grizzly would come his way. If not before dark, then soon after dark. Ned wanted the moment to come before dark when the odds were at least in balance.

About two in the afternoon, the birds fell silent, and even

the gray squirrels vanished. Ned took a deep breath. He felt his horse shudder with fear. The brush was so thick that it crowded him on both sides. The trail was crooked and gave him no open places either in front or in back. The air was chill in shadow, but Ned felt a bead of sweat rolling down his spine. The palms of his hands were clammy with fear. He worried that they might be so wet that they'd not be able to handle the rifle fast enough.

Ned wiped his sweaty palms on his pants legs every few minutes.

Suddenly, his horse reared in terror. Ned grabbed for his saddle horn and looked wildly around for the attack he knew was already underway. The trail was almost overgrown with brush, and when his horse came down on all fours, Ned whirled the animal and saw the three-pawed grizzly which had been tracking him.

The bear was a monster! Saliva made its teeth glisten, and it was a practiced man-killer for it wasted no time in standing on its back legs nor did it roar its warning. Instead, it just charged the man and horse, moving incredibly fast.

The horse bolted sideways into the brush just as Ned unleashed his first bullet. He did not know whether or not his aim was true, and there was no time to do anything but hang on as his horse charged through manzanita and undergrowth. Ned tried to hang on, but huge branches were hanging low. One of them caught him across the face. He felt himself being torn from the saddle and slammed to earth. His face was numb, but he could feel wetness even before he hit the undergrowth. He knew that his nose was smashed into his face.

The Winchester was tangled in the brush. He could hear the horse crashing away through the forest, but nothing mattered except getting his rifle free because the grizzly was coming.

Ned's eyes were blurred. He had lost his hat somewhere, but now he tore the rifle free and levered in another round just as the monster bear appeared. On one knee, oblivious of his broken nose and a broken hip, the old cattleman began to fire as the grizzly bore down at him. Five times the Winchester kicked Ned hard in the shoulder. He was dimly aware that each shot counted, but that it no longer mattered.

The bear would die . . . but not soon enough.

Ned saw the claws raise overhead. As he rolled backward, he unleashed one last bullet that passed up through the grizzly's throat and exited at the base of the monster's skull. Operating on its killer instincts alone, the huge beast fell, striking with its massive paw and scraping one entire side of Ned's face away before its jaws clamped on the rancher's forehead and crushed his skull like an eggshell.

The killer grizzly sank on the man. With its last spark of demented life, it once more tasted the warm, gray mash of human brain.

Michael Cotton drove the wagon into his father's ranch yard. He was shocked to see the rundown condition of the place. All his life, he remembered his father telling him that things had to be kept in good repair. That once a ranch started downhill, it was almost impossible to reverse the spiral. Ned had always preached that a man needed to keep on top of the work or it would crush him one day. As Mike stared around the yard, it was plain that the work had been crushing his father. "I should have stayed and helped," he said aloud to himself.

"What?"

He looked at Nicole. "I said that I should have stayed and worked on this ranch. It looks like hell."

"Looks fine to me," Nicole said. "It's a beautiful place. I had no idea that your father had such a big house. You just said it was made out of logs. I pictured a little cabin."

Mike eased out of the buggy seat to the ground. His ribs and knees were on the mend, but they were still very painful. Oh well, he thought, at least now I'll understand how my patients feel when they receive similar injuries.

"Pa!" he shouted. "You home!"

There was no answer. Mike went to the front door and pushed it open. He moved inside, covering each of the familiar rooms, rooms filled with memories, some good and some bad.

"He's gone," Mike said to Nicole. "Maybe he and the samurai are out gathering cattle and won't be back until after dark."

Nicole studied the big horsehair couch and the fireplace. The room had a chill. "Why don't I get a fire going and see if I can come up with something to eat for when your father and Jessie's samurai return," she said.

"Good idea." Mike walked over to his father's old rolltop desk and lifted the top. He sat down and opened the familiar ledger that he had seen his father work at for so many years. He opened the worn cover and began reading the entries, knowing it would tell the complete story of the bad times that Ned had gone through these past few years while his son was away becoming a doctor.

Mike was not prepared for the desperate figures that he saw. Figures that showed, without a doubt, that his father had been forced to lay off all his riders several years ago and work the huge spread alone. But even then, he'd still kept losing cattle and money. Now, there was little left except the land and a few head of horses and cattle.

"What's wrong?" Nicole asked, seeing the consternation on his face.

"Everything," Mike said, his voice desolate. "All this time

that I was back east going to school I thought that my father was doing well. He wrote letters telling me that things were good, that I didn't need to worry. But he was just covering up, Nicole. He was hanging on by his fingernails until I could finish my medical studies."

Nicole studed the row after row of ledger entries that were so stiff and neat that she could almost sense the nature of the man who had laboriously scratched them onto the pages. She gazed around the room and saw Ned Cotton was a very clean bachelor, one who dusted once or twice a year and who even swept his floors. She wondered if his doctor son was very much like him and decided that he probably was.

"What was it like growing up way out here?" she asked.

He looked up at her. "What do you mean?"

"Did you like it? Didn't you ever miss living near other kids? You know."

"I liked it fine," he said, closing the ledger and leaning back in his father's desk chair. "I was always too busy to miss having friends my own age. My father was my best friend. But there were a lot of others. Back then, we had cowboys in the bunkhouse. They were good men and interested in teaching a kid about horses and cattle. I learned geography from them, too. Texans bragged about their part of the country, while a fella from Montana would be just as fiercely loyal to his part of the country."

Michael shook his head. "I never was bored or lonely. Even after my mother died. But Pa got lonely after my mother passed away. He got so lonely you could see it in his eyes. I used to beg him to sell this spread and come back east with me. I wanted him to live with me near the university while I went to medical school."

"He wouldn't have fit in well at all," Nicole said without

thinking. "I mean . . . he's a Colorado rancher. A man like him would have gotten lost in a big city."

"You're right about that, though I wouldn't admit it for a long time." Michael got up and limped to the window. "I'd like to have a Denver practice and still keep this place," he said. "Keep it for my father and, maybe someday, for my children to pass on to their children."

"I'll bet you have some childhood sweethearts still hanging around these mountains."

He shook his head. "Nope. After I went away, I broke their hearts, and they all married out of spite. None left for me. What about you?"

"You know my story," she said, the smile dying on her lips. "I was Rod Herman's kept girl."

"You ever love him?"

She shrugged. "I guess at first I did. Anyway, his money and things sure turned my head. I saw him as having all the things that I wanted. I figured to get him to marry me, then I'd straighten him out a little. Obviously, neither part of my grand plan worked."

"We never really change people. It almost never works that way. You got to either accept them for what they are or leave 'em alone."

"I'll try to remember that next time," she said.

They looked deep into each other's eyes, then Michael turned his head. "I think I'll go sit on the porch and wait," he said.

Nicole nodded, feeling a lump of disappointment in her throat. It was obvious that he wanted to be alone. Not that she blamed him. It had been a long time since he'd seen his father, and their reunion would be special.

Nicole tossed another log in the fire and wrapped her arms around herself for warmth and comfort. She wished she'd have been one of the Rocky Mountain girls that Mike knew during his childhood. And if he'd have had her for his sweetheart, she'd have waited for him to return no matter how long it took.

In the morning, she awoke and found that the mountains were the quietest place she had ever known. There was no sound of wagons in the street, no cursing teamsters, no whistling storekeepers, or any of the city sounds she had always known.

Nicole climbed out of bed and dressed quickly, then pulled on her shoes and brushed her hair. There was no mirror in the little room he had given her, but she did have a basin of cold water to wash the sleep from her eyes. When she was presentable, she went out into the big living area expecting to find Michael. But he was gone.

For a moment, a shroud of panic dropped over her. The first thing she thought of were those terrible grizzly bears. What if Michael had taken a stroll in the moonlight, been set upon and gobbled without the chance of so much as a warning yip! Why, it might have happened!

Nicole was frantic as she looked around. When she saw Ned Cotton's rifle case, she ran to it and pulled the glass doors aside. The rifles gleamed dully at her, and she was at a loss as to which one she should use. They were all slow and heavy looking, and she wanted something light and shiny.

"Going hunting?" he asked, coming in from the porch where he had spent the night drinking coffee.

Nicole's head snapped up. When she saw he was not dead, she was flooded with joy. She wanted to fly into his arms and tell him how happy she was that a bear did not eat him. Instead, she just swallowed and said, "Good morning, Michael. Did you sleep well?"

He had been watching her curiously. Now, he looked out

the window, and she saw that his face was haggard with worry. "No," he told her. "I didn't sleep at all. Something is wrong, Nicole. Something is *very* wrong."

"What?" Just the tone of his voice gave her the shivers.

"I don't know. It's just a feeling I got in the night. My father and the samurai should have returned, and they did not. I fear something bad has happened to them. I'm going out to find them."

"But you can't! You're a doctor! You know you're not in any fit condition to ride a horse."

"I have to go," he said.

"Then I'm coming too!"

"Not a chance."

"I won't stay here alone!"

Their strong wills clashed. Finally, Michael said, "There's only one horse on the place, the one that pulled us and the buggy up here yesterday."

"Then he'll just have to carry us double."

"Damn but you're stubborn!" he groused.

"Me! You're in awful shape. Busted and cracked ribs. A hurt knee. At least I can walk and ride."

"So can I," he told her. "But I can't seem to lift the damn saddle on the buggy horse. You mind helping?"

Nicole nodded and followed him outside and across the yard to the barn. He had led their buggy horse into the empty hay barn and had found an old stock saddle. But it was heavy, and Nicole could easily see where it would have been too much for a man with broken ribs to lift over the back of a horse. As it was, it took all of her own strength to accomplish the feat. "What do I do now?"

"You have to cinch the horse first, then pull up the chest collar and fasten it through the cinch ring."

"Why do we need a chest collar?"

"To keep the saddle from slipping backwards when we climb mountains," he said. He then showed her how to do everything, and when she was done, he asked her to go into the house and find something to eat so that he could stuff it into the saddlebags for them to take along.

"Uh-uh," she told him right to his face. "The minute I step out of this barn, you'll be riding out the back door, heading for the forest on your own. I see right through you, Michael Cotton."

"You're a suspicious woman," he growled though he did not deny her accusation. "All right then, we'll both go fix a meal to take along. I'll get a rifle too."

So that's how they did it. Twenty minutes later, they were riding across the meadow, following the tracks of Ned Cotton who had followed the samurai.

It was easy to follow Ned Cotton's horse. Even Nicole, who rode behind the cantle of saddle and kept each of her forefingers hooked through the belt loops of Michael's pants, could see the sharp identation of the steel hoof tracks.

When they came to the forest, Michael pulled an old army Colt from his coat pocket. "Do you know how to use one of these?" he asked.

"I think so."

"Good. It's an old cap and ball pistol, and I've loaded all six cylinders with a double dose of gunpowder. If a grizzly attacks and you should fall, then shoot as fast as you can. Those double loads may not stop him, but they'll kill him sooner or later."

"How comforting," she said, taking the heavy revolver and placing it between her hips and the cantle before she rehooked her fingers through his belt loops.

Michael had a huge rifle. "It's a Spencer carbine. It only shoots one bullet before you have to reload, but if you hit a grizzly just right, one bullet is enough. Especially with a double load."

Nicole did not have a response for that. As they rode into the forest, she was so scared she was sure that Michael could hear the trip-hammer sound of her heart.

They rode for hours, Nicole listening to her heart quicken every time some little forest animal made a sound that sent her hand streaking for the big army Colt.

"I bet you wish you'd have stayed back at the ranch," he said.

"No, I don't. It would have been even worse being alone."

"Grizzlies don't usually attack without provocation," Michael said. "I've seen a lot of them up here, and the only time I was ever attacked was by a female who had cubs. I came upon them feeding in a stream just a few miles west of here and it was almost sunset. The cubs scattered and the mother charged."

Nicole waited. "And what happened then?"

"I killed her," Michael said. "With this same rifle. But I wished I hadn't because I know those cubs probably starved to death."

"Maybe they're still alive," Nicole said. "Maybe they're some of the rogue grizzlies that have driven everyone, including your father, out of the basin."

"Maybe," he said. "I've always been fascinated by the animals. I liked to hear stories about them. I know this much, they don't see worth a damn."

"They don't?"

"No. They're like buffaloes; if you remain perfectly still, they can't see you. They can smell you if you're upwind of them, but if you're downwind and still, you're safe. But if they see you and you're close enough, they can charge."

"Upwind. Downwind!" Nicole exclaimed with exasperation. "What sense or good does it do to know that in this kind of timber!"

Michael shrugged. "It is good to know all about your enemies, be they man or beast. What I've just said could, if you didn't panic, save your life."

Nicole laid her cheek against his back. "Just don't get us killed," she pleaded.

Michael said nothing but rode on, every sense alert to danger. When their horse snorted and tried to whirl, Michael thought it was a grizzly. He kicked one leg over the saddle horn and slid to the ground, the big carbine at his shoulder.

But no grizzly came rushing out of the forest to attack. Overhead, the birds were still chattering, so he slowly relaxed and lowered his weapon.

"What is it!" Nicole whispered frantically. "Michael, please get back on this horse and . . ."

Michael disappeared around a bend in the trail up ahead. Nicole's heart almost stopped. She expected to hear a shot and then a cry. Instead, she just heard a deep groan. She slashed the horse across the rump with her revolver and forced the terrified animal forward. When she rounded the bend in the trail, she saw Michael standing with his head bowed beside the dead bear and his horribly mutilated father.

Nicole forgot her own fears and jumped from the horse to run to his side. She tried to grab Michael's face and turn it from the terrible sight, but he was as rigid as a piece of stone. "I'm sorry," she whispered, unable to look at what was left of Ned Cotton's face. "I'm really sorry you found him this way."

"At least he got the one he wanted," Michael said thickly as he motioned toward the missing paw.

He bent down and grabbed his father's arm. He pulled and pulled, but the weight of the monster grizzly was so great that he could not free his father's body until Nicole also helped in the pulling. When they finally got Ned free, Michael looked up for the horse, but it had disappeared.

His expression was gray with sorrow and worry. "We'll bury him now," he said. "Daylight is almost gone, and we don't want to be down here after dark. We'll climb into the trees and bind ourselves tight. In the morning . . ."

He could not finish his words. Nicole looked into his tragic eyes, and then she put her arms around his neck and kissed him on the cheek. For a moment, they clung to each other. Then they pulled apart and set about with the burying.

In the morning, Nicole saw the light of a new day and remembered with a start that she had spent the night tied to a tree trunk some twenty feet above the ground. She could scarcely believe that she had actually fallen asleep, even for a minute.

Michael was still asleep, his body wedged in among the boughs of the pine, his belt looped over a branch. They had both heard a grizzly in the night and had clung to the tree and to each other. Now, with the light coming out of the east, things seemed much less menacing. It seemed to Nicole that, even without a horse, they might be able to escape back down the trail and return to the ranch. After all they had two rifles now, Michael's and the one that his father had used to kill the monster grizzly. And Nicole still had her army Colt stuffed in the pocket of her dress.

She could see the mound of pine needles and fresh dirt where they'd hurriedly buried the rancher. Nicole knew nothing about creatures of the wild, but she suspected that they would dig up the body and devour it. With a horse, they could have tied Ned Cotton across the saddle and maybe gotten him out in one piece. But without a horse, it was all they could do to get themselves out in one piece. It was all her fault.

Nicole turned her eyes away from the grave site and the mound of muscle that was the three-pawed grizzly. She shuddered to think of what a ghastly thing it must have been for Michael's father to die like that. Tears filled her eyes as they had many times in the night. She bit her lip to keep from making a sound and awakening Michael, who was so desperately weary and sad.

Her effort, however, was wasted. "Nicole, don't cry anymore," he said. "It won't help and there's nothing either of us can do now for my father. He was always saying that people should never look back, but only forward."

"I wish I'd have known him," she said. "Do you think . . ."

"Do I think what?"

"Do you think even knowing that I was Rod Herman's mistress that he'd have liked me?"

"Sure he would have!"

"Thank you," she said.

He lifted her chin and kissed her mouth. "If we get out of this mess, I want to marry you, Nicole. I mean that."

"You're crazy!" She would have covered her ears if she hadn't need her hands to keep her grip on the tree. "You don't know me. You don't know what you're saying."

"Yes I do. And I'm afraid that I have something else that's going to sound crazy."

Nicole didn't want to hear it.

"When we get back to the ranch, I'm going to make sure that you're safe. Then I've got to return and find the samurai. He came this way. My father was looking for him and I can do no less."

Nicole could not believe her ears! "Are you insane! Please, you're not thinking straight. You can't come back here! Not after what we've seen."

"I have to."

"Then so do I," she told him. "And there is no sense in wasting a minute's breath in argument."

This time, Michael did not argue.

He's learning, she thought. He's a real fast learner.

Chapter 13

Ki studied the whore named Milly as she waited for George to come rape her again. He could see how her hands clasped tightly together and her face was nearly bloodless with fright.

The samurai sat down beside the slender woman and took her cold hands in his own. For three days and nights, Milly had risked everything to hide him while his strength returned. The cost had been dear, and Ki's own spirit had suffered as George had raped her and then sold her favors to every despicable sonofabitch who had a dollar or two to buy a few minutes' use of her small, punished body. But no more! Now, Ki knew he was able to fight again.

"It's not necessary that you put up with being degraded by him anymore," Ki said quietly. "I will see that it stops."

She had been sitting beside her window, staring out at the nameless town where outlaws and cattle rustlers ruled, and the only law that mattered was the gun on a man's hip. Ki's tranquillity amazed her, gave her strength one minute which eroded into fear the next. She did not understand him, where he had come from or why he seemed so much at peace given the circumstances. Why, if George even imagined how she had helped this wounded stranger. . . . Milly shuddered anew with fear.

"Listen," he said, "George will return soon, and there is no more time. We can leave through the window, or I will kill George and we can leave through the door. It does not matter to me. Which do you want?"

A burst of crazy laughter erupted from her throat. "I don't believe I hear you right! Have you seen anything of George other than his bare ankles from your place under my bed? He's huge and all muscles! He's mean. He likes to hurt me, and he'll like to hurt you as well. And even if we could take him by surprise and kill him, we'd never get out of this town alive."

"Are you finished?" the samurai asked, stroking her cheek. "Because, if you are, I will prepare myself to end your hell."

"No!" She had practically screamed, and he saw that she was almost hysterical. "Look," she pleaded. "I know that you mean well. I understand that you want to help, but the best thing—the only thing—that you can possibly do is just to sneak out after dark and try to get away. If you follow the—"

He placed his hand gently over her lips. "I hear him coming. Please, step back toward the window and try not to look as if you are about to drop through a gallow's trap door."

"You're insane!" she whispered. "He'll kill you, and then he'll beat me to within an inch of my life. Get under the bed!"

Ki stood the woman up before the window. He supposed that, even if he had a week, he would not be able to convince her that he could stand a chance of surviving against a man as big and strong as George.

The samurai's *ninja* outfit had been torn to shreds. He had gotten Milly to find him some western clothing. Even dressed as other men, he did not look like them. His long black hair, his high cheekbones and almond-shaped eyes were all too distinctive. And yet, he was too tall and broad of shoulder to fit the stereotype of an oriental.

Milly's door crashed open. George was already pulling off

his dirty shirt to reveal a thick mat of chest hair. Ki stepped in behind the man and slammed the door shut. He locked the door as George, almost dumb with amazement, looked from one to the other of them. Finally, he bellowed, "Coolie, who the hell are you and whatta you doin' in here with my woman!"

"I am going to punish you for what you have done to Milly," Ki said. "I may even kill you for it."

George stood almost six and a half feet tall and weighed a solid two-forty. Under a massive overhanging ledge of bone, his little eyes blinked as he struggled to comprehend Ki's matter-of-fact statement. When comprehension did dawn on him, he swung around toward Milly and growled, "Have you been givin' it free to this slant-eyed sonofabitch!"

Milly cowered. "I . . . I had no choice. He came here and—"

George raised his hand to strike the woman, but as his arm came down, the samurai sent a vicious sweep kick to the man's kidneys that doubled him up for an instant.

Ki had the big man's full attention now! George roared in pain and whirled around. He advanced with both of his fists moving a lot of air, but the samurai ducked two roundhouse punches and sent a snap-kick to George's crotch that made his mouth form a giant O. Ki filled the O with the hard edge of his hand, and George, hands cupping his ruined testicles, went crashing through the second story window. The scream which filled his throat ended very suddenly.

Ki rushed to the window. "A mistake," he said, looking down at the dead man bathed in shards of glass. "A mistake for certain."

"Hey!" someone yelled, pointing to Ki. "That Chinaman killed Big George!"

For an instant, the men stared at Ki framed in the window.

Then the samurai grabbed Milly's hand and dragged her into the hallway. They raced to the back room and knocked it open. Then Ki locked it behind them saying, "It will take them a few minutes to search and then enter. By then, we'll be in the forest and safe."

"Are you crazy! They have dogs. They'll run us down before we get a mile from here!"

"Is there a river close by!"

"If you call 'close by' five miles! Ki, I'm not going with you. If I stay, I have a chance of talking my way out of everything."

"For what!" he demanded. "So that you can be passed on to someone else to use in the very same manner as George used you?"

"It's better than dying!"

Ki knew that there was no time to explain to Milly the error of her thinking. "I'll be back some day soon," he vowed. "There are stolen cattle here, and I will destroy this town."

"Get out of here!" she cried, racing back to the door and flinging it open.

Ki stopped by the window and looked back once more at her. He shook his head, then he opened the window and jumped into the back alley. He landed as light as a cat and took off running for the trees.

He had to admit that Milly had been right about one thing, she would not have been able to run five miles. And in his weakened state, Ki was not absolutely sure he could either before they overtook him with their dogs.

Even with his shoulder not completely healed and with his body not in its usual perfect condition, Ki was able to run swiftly. Yet, pursuit was also swift. Three miles from the town, he heard the dogs pressing hard on his heels and knew that men on horseback were galloping close behind.

The samurai found a long ledge of rock that spiralled down a steep grade. He followed it closely, hoping that the dogs would not be able to pick up his scent as fast as if he stayed on a dirt trail. When he came to a low, overhanging branch, he swung up on top of it, but paid a hard price as his shoulder wound opened and bled. In considerable pain, he climbed across the tree and then threw himself more than twenty feet down the mountainside to land on a shale slide. The loose rock moved under his feet, and he slid almost ten yards down to a stump burned out by lightning. Ki grabbed a piece of charred wood and smeared it on the soles of his shoes, and then he bounded down the mountain and disappeared into the trees. His evasive actions just might have given him enough time to reach the river.

Once, he caught his foot in a twisted root and fell heavily. The only thing that kept him from landing squarely on his bad shoulder was his superb reflexes. He climbed to his feet just as the first rifle shot chipped a piece of stone near his leg, and then Ki dashed onward.

He did not look back for he knew that everything depended upon his reaching the water and diving into its swift torrent. The shots started coming in bursts, and they richocheted off the rocks and whined meanly all about him. Ki continued to run as hard and as fast as he could. The river was just up ahead.

The first of the hounds overtook him about fifty yards from the water. It was a big dog, and it sank its fangs into the meat of the samurai's calf muscle. Ki almost fell. He tried to kick the dog away, but it hung on until the edge of the samurai's hand slashed down and struck the beast just behind the ear. The vicious leader of the pack crumpled and began to howl in pain; his behavior sent the rest of the dogs into a state of confusion.

Ki finally did look back to see the riders driving their horses through the swirling dogs. The samurai managed a tight grin; then he executed a running dive that sent him far out into the racing river. The current was swift and the water was deep. Fortunately, Ki had entered a stretch where there were few big boulders. He was able to swim underwater for several minutes before he surfaced a long way down from where he had entered the water.

He saw the riders, took another deep breath and ducked back beneath the current which swept him around a bend and carried him into a gorge. When Ki surfaced again, he looked back and knew he had eluded his pursuers. When he glanced up ahead, his heart almost stopped for he was being swept toward a thundering waterfall. He had no idea how high it might be but knew that he had to assume he would be killed if he plunged over the edge.

Ki spotted a fallen log wedged across some boulders and swam hard for it. Ignoring his bad shoulder, he lunged out of the water just as the current was dragging him toward the falls. For a moment, he was sure that the river was going to pull him under the log and send him to his death. His entire lower body was whipped under the log. He struggled desperately to hang on and drag himself free of the current.

Inch by inch, the samurai bested the river until, finally, he was able to pull himself up high enough to throw one leg over the mossy log. He lay still for several minutes, shaken, weak and grateful to be alive. When he felt stronger, he climbed to his feet and stood on the log. He was able to see that the waterfall dropped only about eight feet into a huge pool.

Ki expelled a deep breath. There was no way to reach either bank so he just jumped back into the river and let its force sweep him over the waterfall. He realized that the force of the water might drive him into rocks below and kill him, but there was little choice but to take that chance.

Tons of water drove him right to the bottom of the pool, and it tried to squeeze the air from his lungs. Ki was, however, able to swim along the rocky floor of the pool until he could plant his feet and propel himself up to the surface. Breath held too long exploded from his burning lungs, and then he inhaled the sweet, pine-scented air and allowed the water to carry him to the edge of the pool. He crawled up on the warm sand and closed his eyes.

He was safe. He would sleep for awhile. Then he would figure out how to make his way back to Ned Cotton. Once there, they would go straight to Denver and find Jessie. There they could rouse a posse and return to wipe out the outlaw stronghold.

There was much to do. The samurai's hand touched his shoulder, and he hoped that he had not lost too much more blood and strength. The real fighting was yet to come.

Chapter 14

Rod Herman waited impatiently behind his desk. He kept tapping his pencil on his desk blotter and glancing up at the door until the knock he had been waiting for finally sounded.

"Come on in!" he barked.

Wes and three other men trooped into his office. They were dusty from a long ride into the mountains, and their faces were drawn with fatigue. It was Wes, the hatchet-faced man who made their report.

"We found 'em all right. Just like you said. Mike Cotton and Nicole are at the ranch."

The pencil snapped in Herman's powerful fist. He had not forgotten the beating and humiliation he'd taken at the hands of the young doctor. He was festering inside to get even. "Who else?"

"No one. Ned Cotton was killed by Old Three Paws."

Herman jerked forward in his chair. "What!" he exclaimed.

"The grizzly killed Ned Cotton. Then the bear died. Mike Cotton and Nicole found their bodies. That's all there is to tell," Wes drawled. "I figured you'd be glad."

"Did you actually see the body!" Herman demanded. "There are plenty of fools running around up there trying to collect a grizzly bounty."

Wes was not easily disturbed, but he had seen the body. It

was not something he much wanted to remember or talk about. "I seen what was left of Ned. He still had enough face on him to tell. There's no mistake, boss."

Herman leaped out of his chair. He was beaming. "That's the best news I've had in a long time. My only regret is that Ned killed Old Three Paws before I could claim him for a trophy. You know, I'm the one that shot off that back paw years ago and made him wild. I did it on purpose, but I never expected it to work out so well."

"That bear was sure a big bastard," one of the gunman drawled. "He was biggern a draft horse. Stinkin' pretty bad by the time we got there."

Herman did not give a damn about that. "Jessie had a friend. A very dangerous friend, from what I am told. He's a samurai."

"A what?" Wes said.

"A samurai. They're an ancient order of fighting men from the Orient. They use . . . oh, hell, I don't know. Strange weapons. Sticks and crazy blades and stuff."

"Ain't nothing that can stand up to Mr. Colt and Mr. Winchester," Wes said. "What does this guy look like?"

"He looks like a coolie, only he's bigger. I understand he's half Japanese and half white man."

"He's half way to the grave if he steps in our way," one of the gunmen promised. "What about Mike Cotton and Nicole? You gonna let 'em get away with anything?"

Herman looked at Wes. "Do you remember what I said I was going to do to that girl?"

"You said you'd give her to the Apache," Wes replied. "I remembered that because I figured it would be worse for a woman than death."

"That's the way I figure it too," Herman said. "That's why we're going up to the ranch."

"You mean you're coming too?"

"Yeah," Herman said. "I wouldn't miss it for anything. I'm going to take a little vacation, and we're all going to New Mexico."

"What about Mike Cotton?"

"He's going somewhere too," Herman said with a smile. "He's going to join his old man in hell."

The men laughed. Herman passed out cigars and then poured them all drinks from his stock of imported whiskey. They raised their glasses in a toast, and Herman said, "To long journeys and mean, lustful Apache!"

The men laughed again. All together. Then, they drank to Herman's toast and started talking about how soon they could leave again.

"You boys get some food and sleep," Herman said. "We'll leave after dark. I don't want anyone to see me on the way out. If we ride hard, we'll be at the ranch by daybreak, just in time to surprise Cotton and Nicole. If I know her, she's screwing the doctor's brains out right now."

Nicole stepped into his bedroom and closed the door behind her. She stared at the young doctor who stood in the shadows. "I could hear you pacing the floor. You've been doing it night after night. You've got to get some sleep, Mike."

"I can't," Mike said. "I've tried. But I just can't. I keep seeing my father's face. I'm afraid that if I close my eyes, I'll wake up screaming."

Nicole moved to him. She had never been in love before. She'd been infatuated, awed and impressed, but never in love. Not like this. She put her arms around his neck and drew his face to the man's nightshirt she wore.

He groaned and his arms came around her girlish hips. His fingers caressed her firm buttocks. "Nicole," he whispered, picking her up and carrying her to the bed he had not lain in since discovering his father's body.

She pulled him down beside her, feeling his breath warm on her neck. Then he reached under the nightshirt and stroked her body. She shivered with excitement and rolled over onto him. She unbuttoned his pants and shoved them and his underclothes down to his ankles.

"I need you," he whispered. "You don't know how much I need you."

"Tell me!" she said, urgent with need for someone to finally love her. "No one has ever needed me for anything but my body."

"I do. I need you for strength," he said, feeling her lips trail down his belly and then slide over his stiffening manhood. He felt her hot mouth take him inside of her, and he finally closed his eyes and did not see the half-face of his poor father. "I need you for hope and for love."

Her mouth seemed to need him too as it worked up and down his erect shaft, polishing it in the moonlight that shone through his window. She raised her head. "How else, Michael?"

"I need you like the sun and the stars and the moon and the clean air. I need you like I need my very breath!"

Her head dipped and he shuddered. His hips were moving as she milked him expertly. When he could stand the pleasure no longer, he drew her up to him, and they kissed deeply, tongues and bodies pushing hard at each other. Before he quite realized it, she was opening for him like the petals of a rosebud. He moved strongly into her. She moaned, her fingernails stroking his lean buttocks and gently pulling him as deep as he could go.

"If I could die like this," she panted, surging up and down with him, "I wouldn't mind at all."

He buried himself in her completely. It was easy to lose himself in her hair and her smell and her heat. Michael took his time with this woman for they had a lifetime to give each other pleasure. Almost an hour later, when he could control his body no longer, he took her in a series of hard thrusts that brought them both a thundering climax that seemed as if it would never end.

"I love you," he said. "I don't give a damn what you have done or been. That's all in the past. All that matters now is the future."

"Can we stay here forever. Stay right in this bed?"

He chuckled. "We'd starve."

She grew serious. "Can we at least keep this ranch and live here some of the year? It will be our getaway. Our place in the sun. The place where we can conceive our children and watch them grow strong."

"Yes," he said. "But I'll have to kill the grizzly bears first."

"Maybe they'll go away," she said, now drowsy with sleep, her physical exhaustion brought on by their long and vigorous lovemaking. "Maybe they'll all just go away."

"Maybe," he told her, kissing her lips softly. But he did not believe it.

When she was sound asleep, he rolled out of bed and dressed. He went into the living room, opened the gun case and removed the buffalo rifle. It was already loaded, so he stepped out into the night and started across the moonlit basin.

Yesterday, he'd seen another dead steer at the far end of basin. A steer obviously slaughtered by a grizzly. From the signs he had seen since returning, he was sure that only one rogue bear was killing the last of his father's stock. If it returned for yesterday's kill, he would shoot it and put an end to the killer grizzlies. The rest of them must have moved deeper into the wilderness when the cattle, sheep and horses were mostly all gone.

Just one more, he thought. And then I can make it safe for Nicole and our children. Safe for as long as we may live.

Rod Herman dismounted behind the haybarn and led his men forward. He fully expected to take Mike Cotton and Nicole without a shot being fired. With Wes and four other gunmen at his flanks, there was little risk of dying.

He moved quickly across the yard and up to the front porch. He motioned for his men to split up and move around the house so that no one escaped. Then, he stood back while Wes opened the front door, gun in hand, narrow face tense and body half-crouched.

Wes hurried soundlessly inside. They split up then and began to tiptoe through the rooms. Herman was in luck. He found Nicole first, but she was alone.

For a long moment, he stared at her in the moonlight, wanting her again. He had never had a woman that was any better than Nicole when she was in the right mood. And she had usually been in the right mood. He could feel himself stiffen with desire as she lay there on the rumpled bed, as peaceful and innocent appearing as a child.

"I didn't find nobody. . ."

Wes' words trailed off. "Well look at that!" He looked hopefully at his boss. Rod Herman knew what he wanted. "Any sign of Cotton?" he whispered.

"He's gone."

Herman looked back at Nicole, and then he nodded his head. "Go ahead and take her," he said, "I'll send the other men in one by one."

Wes was fast with a gun and faster with a woman. Before

Herman was even out the door, he had his gunbelt off and was shucking out of his pants. Herman left Nicole's bedroom door open.

He wanted to hear her scream.

An hour later, the sun was coming over the Continental Divide, bright as a newly minted penny. Nicole sat slumped on her horse. Every one of the men had used her, and still she had refused to tell Rod where Mike had gone. In the end, they had dragged her out of the bed and thrown her onto a horse. Still in the man's nightshirt, still barefooted and crying.

"Let's go," Herman said with anger. "Let's find us some Apache and make a trade!"

The men laughed. Nicole was too numb to understand as her horse was whipped into a gallop and she was carried away.

Chapter 15

Only a few miles away, Michael Cotton sat crouched in the rocks with his big Sharps. He could see the first light of dawn coming up, and he knew that the killer grizzly would be near and probably ready to feed on his earlier kill. Michael had not gone near the kill during the night, for that would have alerted the grizzly to danger and might have sent the big animal deeper into the forest. Grizzlies were unafraid of man, but they were also very smart. Those that still lived generally kept out of a man's rifle sights.

Michael took a deep, ragged breath. His eyes burned for lack of sleep, and there was a slight tremor in his hand. He needed some time to adjust himself to the horror that he had seen on his father's face. He needed to shift his thinking to Nicole. To caring for her and loving her and making her his wife.

He had no illusions about Nicole's questionable past nor about the stigma that would come upon him when he married the former mistress of one of Denver's wealthiest and most powerful citizens. People would talk. Some would shun his medical practice and make it harder for him to get established. But Denver was growing fast, and new people were coming in every day. If the old line wanted to hold it against him for marrying Nicole, then he would do just fine without them . . . he hoped.

Michael closed his eyes for a moment. The next thing he knew, he was jerking his head back up. The sun had floated clear of the divide. But he hardly noticed because right at the edge of the clearing was the grizzly. It was coming towards him, snout up in the air.

Michael knew at a glance that the wind had shifted in the past hour that he had been sleeping. He was now upwind of the grizzly, and it had his scent. The huge creature was no more than three hundred yards away, coming in that shuffling way with its head wagging back and forth like a fat finger.

The grizzly was really quite beautiful. It was a silver tip, and every hair shone in the bright morning sun. Michael stood up in the rocks. The bear caught his movement and began to charge. Mike took aim and fired. A huge cloud of white smoke billowed out in front of him, and he had to squint to see the grizzly.

His marksmanship had not entirely deserted him though he had made far better shots. The heavy lead ball hit the grizzly in the chest and stopped it. The beast rolled over pawing at its chest and then came on again.

Michael fought down his own panic as he began to reload. His father had always said that a man was a fool to expect that he could kill a grizzly with one bullet. You needed to give yourself at least two shots with anything smaller than a cannon. Michael began to reload. He hauled a paper-wrapped cartridge out of his pocket, which he had already made with an extra charge of black powder and a .52 caliber ball. Forcing himself not to panic as his hands moved clumsily because he had not practiced with the carbine in so many years, Michael pulled back the big side hammer and slid the block up to expose the chamber. Then, he shoved the paper-wrapped cylinder into the chamber and levered the breech block into place knowing that, on the way down, a sharp edge of the breech block would slice off the back end of the paper cartridge. He fumbled with the cap, dropped it in the dirt, retrieved it and took aim again.

The badly wounded grizzly wasn't moving quite as fast as before but it was still faster than any man could run. Michael wanted to aim for the bear's forehead, but that was too risky a shot. So he went for the heart again. But to his horror, the cap did not ignite the powder.

Michael tore the cap off with his fingernails and replaced it with another. The grizzly was less than fifty yards away now, and he shot too fast. His ball hit the pain-crazed beast in the shoulder with enough force to knock it sideways, but the bear just bawled and kept coming.

Michael knew that he was a dead man if he tried to reload again. There just was not enough time. He had hoped this would not happen, but he had tried to prepare himself for any eventuality. Slinging the Sharps over his shoulder, he jumped up onto the rocks and climbed to their top. He was sure the grizzly could and would come up after him. There was a tall, lodgepole pine close by, and so he jumped for it. Unfortunately, the limb he grabbed was old and brittle. It snapped off at the trunk and he dropped two feet before he was able to grab more branches and hang on. He shimmied around on the far side of the pine and struggled upward.

The bear had already scaled the rocks. Now, it leaned out toward the lodgepole pine, using one paw to rip at the tree. Michael was about two feet beyond its grasp, and the mortally wounded grizzly roared in anger and dropped to the earth. It gripped the slender pole in his mighty arms and shook the tree hard. Michael hung on for dear life.

Failing to dislodge him, the huge grizzly tried to climb the tree. From the way it started out, it seemed to Michael that he was as good as dead.

Fumbling in the upper branches, half-strangled by his own sling, he somehow managed to reload. Then he fired straight down into the jaws of the snarling beast.

White smoke billowed up around the tree, and when it cleared, he looked down to see the dead grizzly.

Michael did not trust himself to come down but clung to the branches, his body bathed in fear-sweat.

"You can't stay up there all day," Ki said. "So you might as well come down."

Michael opened his eyes to see the samurai standing on the rocks below. He sighed. "Boy am I glad to see you!" Then added. "Why didn't you help me?"

"You were doing fine on your own. Besides, that's the only tree close by, and I thought it looked a little crowded."

Michael shook his head and shinnied down the lodgepole. He found that his knees were so weak that they wanted to buckle. "Would you have done anything if the grizzly had reached me?"

"Yes," the samurai said. "I was trying to decide what. I've no rifle or bow and arrows. Only this knife."

Michael shook his head. "You could have shoved it up his ass, but that would only have sent him up the tree faster."

Ki grinned. He steadied the young doctor, studying his condition. "We are both in pretty poor shape," he said. "Where's your father?"

"He's dead," Michael said. "He was killed by the three-pawed bear, but it went down with him."

Ki turned away. He guessed he shouldn't have left the old rancher and gone off alone. Maybe if he'd stayed that man would still be alive. "What about Miss Starbuck?"

"She's still in Denver. She told me to tell you that everything was all right. That she was going to meet with her attorney, and they'd find some way to block the sale."

"I found a cattle rustler's town," Ki said. "It's about fifty miles southwest of here, deep in the mountains. The grizzlies have had a lot of help in taking away your livestock."

Michael's eyes widened. "You say a whole town?"

"Yes." The samurai thought of Milly and his promise. "As soon as I can, I'm going back for someone. I figured you and a posse might also like to come along."

"I doubt the sheriff would go," Michael said, as he turned and they started back toward the ranchhouse. "You see, it's out of his jurisdiction. He never has been one to go to any more trouble than was absolutely necessary."

"Doesn't sound like much of a man."

"He's not." Michael said, trudging along. "I got a girl with me, Ki. She was Rod Herman's woman, but that can't be held against her anymore. When the chips were down, she came with me and Miss Starbuck. I can't wait for you to meet her!"

Ki looked sideways at the young docor. "You seem pretty excited."

"I'm going to marry her."

"You sure you aren't rushing it a little?"

"Nope. This is not the first one I've kissed, but she's the last. Ki, it's like we've known each other forever."

The samurai didn't say anything. To his way of thinking, Michael might be a little rash, but that was his business. Politics. Love. Religion. There were the three things that a wise man avoided arguing about. They were all highly emotional issues. Too emotional to discuss rationally.

When they reached the ranchhouse, Michael bounded inside and yelled, "Nicole! Come and meet an old friend. A samurai!"

There was no answer. Michael hurried through the house,

and when he came back outside, he found the samurai down on one knee, studying horse tracks.

"Ki, she's gone!"

The samurai looked up at the stricken face of the young doctor. "I know," he said. "She's been carried away."

"By who!"

Ki moved into the house. He found the bedroom, and his eyes told him the story of how the girl had been repeatedly raped and then dragged out to a horse. He would not tell Michael what his eyes could not deny.

"Well," Michael said. "Do you have any idea what happened!"

"She was kidnapped by five men. They rode south."

Michael groaned. "We don't even have horses to go after them!"

The samurai knew that he was not strong enough to overtake the men and their captive on foot and neither was the injured doctor. "Then we must find horses and weapons," he said.

"We'll have to go damn near to Denver for 'em."

"Then," the samurai said, "we might as well find Jessie and tell her what has gone wrong."

Chapter 16

Ki could have traveled much faster without Michael, but he did not want to leave the young doctor behind. So he walked slowly and rested often because Michael's knee was giving him fits.

"This is no good," Michael said after he had limped about seven miles. He slumped down in the shade of a pine tree, face white with pain. "Ki, I'm slowing you down too much. You go on ahead. Find Miss Starbuck and get us some horses and provisions, then stop back at the ranch for me. I'll rest and get this knee in shape for a long ride."

"All right," Ki said, because he knew it was the best thing to do. "We will be back as soon as possible."

Michael looked extremely dejected. "I should never have left Nicole," he said. "Because of that, she's gone."

Ki studied the sky. He still had to hike over the divide. It was going to be a long pull. To the east, he could see big thunderheads building over what he imagined would be Denver. He hoped it did not rain in the mountains because that would make tracking the kidnappers that much more difficult.

"Ki?"

The samurai turned to the doctor.

"Ki, do you ever make mistakes? My father said you were damn near infallible."

"Not true. I made a terrible mistake by leaving your father. If I had stayed with him he would be alive. If I'd returned instead of followed a cattle rustler, he'd also be alive. I make mistakes," Ki told the disconsolate man. "But what good does that do either one of us? All that is required of anyone is that they do their best. That and to act with honor and to be humble in victory and gracious in defeat. We can do no more than that."

Michael nodded. "You're right, of course. But I just can't stop thinking about Nicole. If they harm her—"

"We'll kill them either way," Ki said, knowing that the men *had* harmed Nicole. He'd seen no blood, but she had been abused and more than once.

"Be ready," the samurai told the doctor. "For I will return with the others very soon."

With those words, Ki left the man and settled into a long, swinging stride that would carry him over the Continental Divide and then down to Denver.

Ki ran all that evening. During the night, he alternately walked and ran, measuring out his strength very carefully so that by the time he reached Denver, he was running on pure courage. He raised more than a few eyebrows as he staggered up the street and stumbled into the hotel. The clothes Milly had stolen for him were filthy and torn from the brush along the narrow game trails he had followed. When Francois saw him, he was shocked. "My God!" he exclaimed. "You look as if you have run a hundred miles!"

Ki had run a hundred miles when he added in the distance to the outlaw town. "Is Miss Starbuck in her room?"

Francois nodded. "She is, but I think it would be best to slip a note under her door."

When the Frenchman winked, Ki understood. "Then do it," he said. "I must see her immediately."

Francois wrote a note and passed it to a clerk with the necessary instructions. "Just slip the note under the door and knock, but do not wait for a reply," Francois explained.

The hotel clerk hurried upstairs.

Francois turned to the samurai with concern in his voice. "My friend," he said. "Even you must rest."

"There is no time for rest."

"Then time must be made," Francois said. "Jessie has a room waiting for you. Why don't you go upstairs and rest for a few minutes. I'll send a bath, fresh clothes, and nourishment."

Ki said, "I must tell you that Nicole is in trouble."

The Frenchman's hand fluttered to his mouth. "Is she . . . dead?"

"No. She has been kidnapped from the Cotton Ranch. I don't know who or even why."

Francois' face turned almost scarlet. "It must be that animal Rodney Herman! Who else but a jilted lover would harm such an innocent flower?"

"It will be easy to find out if he is in town or not," Ki said. "After that, we can decide what is best."

"There is only one thing to do!" Francois cried. "I must kill him! It is a matter of honor."

Ki knew that Frenchmen were very proud and that their honor was as sacred to them as it was to a samurai. However, unlike samurai, Frenchmen tended to be hot-tempered and sometimes quite illogical. "You must not think of killing the man. If there is killing to be done, then I shall do it."

"That is impossible!" Francois cried. "Nicole is *my* responsibility, not yours!"

Jessie was rushing down the staircase. She studied the

weariness in Ki's face and the strange clothes he was wearing. She could see dried blood from his shoulder wound, and she was shocked by his haggard appearance. "Ki, what is wrong?"

The samurai told her quickly, without embellishments or dramatics and without digressing from the facts. That was the way Jessie liked to receive information. As soon as he was finished, Jessie sent a clerk with a note for Quentin and said, "We must leave at once. I am sure that Nicole was taken by Rod Herman. The man was insane with jealousy and humiliated right here in the dining room when he was soundly whipped by Michael Cotton."

Michael had not told the samurai of his fight, but it explained why Herman would seek vengeance against the girl. His enormous pride would have tipped him to the brink of insanity. "I will be ready to leave within two hours. Are my bow and arrows in my room?"

"Yes," Jessie said. "Everything you need is there. But is your shoulder fit to pull the bow?"

"I will be by the time we catch up with those we seek," Ki told her.

Francois pushed forward. "I have to come with you," he said. "There is no choice for me. It is a matter of honor."

"You don't know what you're asking," Jessie told the little Frenchman. "We'll be riding hard and over a long distance. Whoever has taken Nicole commands a huge lead. There will be hundreds of miles to cover. When we finally overtake those who kidnapped Nicole, they might have already killed her."

The hotel owner's lower lip quivered. "Without honor, a Frenchman is dead," he said with great conviction. "If you insist on leaving without me, then I will follow you. I can shoot a gun."

Jessie's eyes met those of the samurai. She could tell by looking at Ki that he understood they could not leave this man behind without killing something in him. "All right," she said. "We leave in two hours. We will need the best horses, saddles and equipment I can buy in this town. Francois, you will also need warm clothing. A rifle along with plenty of ammunition. A hat. A coat and a rainslicker. A bedroll and riding clothes, including boots. We will need food and supplies."

"I will take care of the food," the Frenchman said. "I will bring good cheeses, wines and—"

"No," Jessie sighed, "I just don't think you understand what kind of an ordeal this is going to be."

The Frenchman bristled. "If it is torture, all the more reason to bring many bottles of good wine."

"We'll be traveling fast," Jessie said. "That means light. There will be no time to drink wine in crystal glasses. You don't seem to realize what we are facing out there."

Francois looked crestfallen. "I will become austere," he declared. "Leave the food preparations to me."

Jessie had her misgivings, but she had so many details to settle before they left that she really did need the Frenchman's help. "All right. But you must remember, anything that you bring must be small and light or it will slow your horse down. It's your niece that we are trying to rescue."

Quentin Daily came hurrying into the hotel lobby. He looked at Jessie and said, "Mr. Herman has vanished. Just completely disappeared from town. His clerk will tell me nothing."

"Ah ha!" Francois cried. "I told you!"

Jessie nodded. "All right then. It does seem that the attorney and his men have taken things into their own hands. So it is up to us to catch them." She looked at Quentin and then turned toward the samurai and introduced the pair.

"Quentin believes he has found a small loophole in the law. He will remain here in Denver and expand the loophole so that when we return, we can save the ranch for Ned and—"

Ki took a deep breath. Then he explained that Ned Cotton had been killed by the grizzly.

"Damn," Jessie whispered. She looked at the attorney. "Quentin, what happens now?"

"It changes nothing," Quentin said. "The law is fairly clear in this regard. Since Ned is gone, everything that he would have been entitled to now goes to his son, Michael." The attorney touched her arm. "Jessie, I insist on going along too."

Jessie took a deep breath and expelled it slowly. "Can you shoot a gun well?"

"I'm no gunfighter, but I can handle one."

"All right then. We go together, and we stay together until we track down Rod Herman and his men even if we have to ride all the way to Mexico."

They all nodded. As Jessie looked at each of their faces, she saw determination. "I think we'll be all right when we catch up with them," she said. "They are gunmen, but they won't be expecting a chase."

"But how can we be sure we can stay on their trail?" Francois asked. "One hard rain and it is gone."

Ki had the answer to that. "If we lose it, we separate for awhile and keep riding. Sooner or later, if they stick to one direction, we'll find them. I promise you that."

"I want to kill Herman," Francois announced. "That is my right."

Jessie just shook her head with exasperation. It was clear that Francois was going to be the unstable link in their line of pursuit and attack. But at least he had the heart of a lion. And sometimes even incompetent men who faced odds far beyond their capabilities succeeded on nothing more than a little luck and a lot of grit. Jessie had the feeling there was no shortage of grit in her men, but there was no doubt they would also need some luck.

"Let's go," she said. "I'll buy the horses and tack and have everything out in front in less than two hours. Then, we ride."

"Ki?"

The samurai turned as he started toward his room. His mind was already on his bow and arrows. It would be good to have them with him this time.

"Ki, how is Michael's health?"

"He'll make it if we have to tie him across the saddle," Ki said.

"And the girl. You're holding back on me. Why?"

"Because of Francois. The man is upset enough without knowing that his niece was raped by all of Herman's men."

Jessie's eyes tightened. "She is strong, Ki. I like her strength. And if we can overtake them while she yet lives, I think she will be all right."

"There is only one reason he would take her," the samurai said. "It is that he wants to see her suffer."

"I agree. Then where are they going?"

Ki expelled a deep breath. "I cannot say for sure. But if you wanted a woman to go through a living hell, where would you take her?"

"South," Jessie answered without hesitation. "South toward the Arizona Territory and the Apache or maybe the Comanchero."

Ki nodded. "Exactly."

"God help her if we don't reach her in time," Jessie said, turning and walking away.

While Jessie and Quentin bought horses, saddles and all

the other equipment that they would need for the long chase, the samurai bathed, ate and then meditated. Just before the end of two hours, he stood up and gathered up his bow and quiver with its special arrows. The samurai replaced the *shur-iken* star blades he had spent and also the *surushin*.

He was clean, and now his mind was fresh even though his body was not. He was ready to lead the search for Nicole. When he walked out of his room, down the steps and out to the street, Jessie had a horse ready for him.

"I've a spare for Michael," she said, pointing to a saddled horse. "But where is Francois?"

"Here I am!" he called, riding a horse and leading another pack horse around from behind his hotel.

Jessie stared at the pack horse. Obviously, the Frenchman had not been able to get all of the food he'd wanted to take on his own animal, so he'd hired an extra horse. The pack horse was a good looking animal, and Jessie decided that it would not slow them down. Still, she could see the suspicious out-lines of many wine bottles.

The hell with it, she thought. A Frenchman is not a Frenchman without wine, cheese and his honor.

Chapter 17

When they reached the Cotton Ranch, Michael was ready. Being a doctor, he'd taped his ribs and his injured knee was tightly wrapped. "I won't be able to run any races," he said. "But I'll be able to ride until my horse drops."

The young physician was grim, and he looked fit enough to ride to the end of the earth if necessary. Jessie rested the men and the horses for three hours. Then they started south with Ki in the lead, tracking the kidnappers. The trail led down through the magnificent San Juan Valley and then joined the Rio Chama River near its headwaters and followed it south. Always south.

After several more days of hard riding, they neared the historic town of Santa Fe. Michael, having been raised on horseback, was in good shape despite his knee and ribs. But Quentin was the son of a Pennsylvania coal miner, and he was raw from the saddle. Francois felt even worse. It was clear that he was in agony from the long days and nights on horseback. And now, as they rested their horses just a few miles north of Santa Fe, the Frenchman was pulling out another bottle of French wine, his only relief against the fire of his raw flesh.

"Francois," Jessie said, taking the man aside so that they could speak privately. "I need a special favor of you."

The Frenchman's heart was willing, but he was so beaten that he could barely nod his head. "Anything," he sighed, upending the bottle and drinking it without the benefit of a crystal glass. Something he would never have thought he'd stoop to do.

Jessie knew the Frenchman could not go much farther. "As you know, Santa Fe is just up ahead. It is a town where the lawless are to be found. I should not be surprised if Rod Herman and his men were there still."

Francois had been wondering how he would ever make it to Apache country where the Indians could, with his full permission, put him out of his misery. But only after he had killed Herman. Now, he found that his spirits were suddenly being restored.

"You mean . . . you mean we really might not have to go any farther?"

"Exactly. But I need your help."

"I will do anything!"

"Good." Jessie looked into Francois' pain-reddened eyes. "I need you to remain right here with your rifle in case we flush them out of town, and they double back."

Francois was a little drunk, but not so drunk that Jessie's words did not cause him confusion. "But why would they do that?"

"I don't know. But it is likely that Herman and his men were involved with the cattle rustling. If that is the case, they might well try to reach the outlaw town where they could regroup and then overwhelm us. You cannot let them do this."

The Frenchman nodded his head. It made sense to him. It seemed he was being asked to do something very important. It was an honorable commission. "I could do this," he said. "I could find a place where they would not see me. I could stop them from escaping."

Jessie clapped his shoulder. "I knew that you could be counted upon. That's why I specifically asked you to do this very important job."

Francois' chin lifted. He forced a grin and said proudly, "I will not fail you. But what if they chose to run farther south?"

Jessie nodded gravely. "That is a possibility," she admitted. "If it happens, you must wait for us in Santa Fe. If we are caught in a trap and annihilated, you will be the only one that can exact revenge . . . for all of us. Without that, our memories will have been dishonored."

"I see! Yes, I understand!"

"Good," Jessie said. What she had told Francois was very unlikely to happen, but she knew the Frenchman would buy it. And, in truth, there was a slight but real possibility that Rod Herman might sell or trade Nicole in Santa Fe and start back toward either Denver or the outlaw town that Ki had found.

Ki located a fine spot overlooking the main northern trail into Santa Fe. The spot was near a small creek where both Francois' saddle and pack horses could drink. There was also enough grass to last the two animals a week, plenty of shade and a magnificent view. Ki helped the Frenchman unpack a half dozen bottles of French wine and a huge chunk of cheese and two loaves of bread. It looked like the man was settled in for an extended picnic. "You have everything you need. If I were you, I'd lay in that cool stream for a few hours. It will help those saddle sores if you make a poultice by packing a little moss inside your pants."

Francois looked appalled by the idea, so the samurai said nothing more and rode away.

"I just hope that I'm doing the right thing," Jessie said when they were well out of hearing. "If Rod Herman and his men were actually to get past us and—"

"Don't even think it," Quentin said.

"That's right," Michael added. "Besides, Francois was in such agony that he could not have gone any farther. What you did was the humane thing. He'll spend a couple of days drinking the rest of his wine and finishing up his food. Then he'll get hungry and decide to come into Santa Fe. By then, we'll be a hundred miles south. He was slowing us down."

"Now I'll be the one that will slow you down," the attorney complained bitterly. "I just never had the chance to get used to riding a horse. Back in the coal country, the only people who owned horses were rich."

"Just do the best you can," Jessie told the man. "And keep your eyes open for trouble and your gun ready."

"Do you really think they might be here?"

"I think that's a real possibility," Jessie said. "A man like Rod Herman must realize that his life would be in real danger in Apache country. And while I haven't been in Santa Fe for more than five years, the last time I was here, there was slave trafficking. Comancheros, white outlaws and Mexican banditos were buying and selling women. It made me sick to think about it, but the practice is centuries old. It's hard to stamp out."

Quentin shook his head. "And here I thought slavery had been abolished by President Abraham Lincoln's Emancipation Proclamation of 1863."

"In the South it had an effect, but not down here," Jessie said. "Mostly, the slaves are Indian or Mexican women and girls stolen from little villages and camps. There are no laws to protect them except Colt's law."

"Maybe this part of the country needs a good lawyer," Quentin said. "One that can make some changes."

Jessie looked at the man. "I think they could. If you're interested in a little help to get you started, I've got some land down here that I am thinking of developing into a horse ranch, but there are some legal details that need to be addressed."

Quentin shook his head. "Jessie," he said. "The day I find a place that you *don't* have land is the day I'll be in for a surprise. But I'll say this, I sure am glad to see a town again. And I hope that Herman and his men are still there. If this is going to come down to guns, I'd just as soon do it now as later."

As they neared the old frontier town, Jessie thought about its long history. Santa Fe had been founded by the Spanish in 1610 on the banks of the Santa Fe River, a small tributary of the Rio Grande. The words Santa Fe meant "Holy Faith," and the city had been the hub and trading center of the southwest ever since its founding. Now, as Jessie and her friends rode into town, they saw that the old plaza with its sparkling fountain and stately trees looked as cool and inviting as ever.

But Jessie, Ki, Michael and Quentin were too intent on their business to enjoy the relaxed Spanish flavor of the town. They tied their horses at one end of the town and checked their guns.

Jessie laid it out for everyone. "Ki and I will take that side of the street," she said pointing. "Quentin, you and Mike take the other. If you see Rod Herman or any of his gunmen, try not to be seen until we all regroup."

Quentin wore his gun in a shoulder holster under his coat. "Shall we ask questions?"

"Not until we've searched the town from top to bottom," Jessie said. "If they're here and they learn someone is looking for them, it will be ten times harder to rescue Nicole. Let's see if we can get her before any shooting starts."

Michael nodded his head. "That has to be our first concern," he said as they split up. "No matter what, we have to save Nicole."

Nicole had been locked in the Santa Fe hotel room for almost a week, always with a guard. She saw Rod Herman every day, but he would not speak to her. It was only from one of the guards that she learned he was waiting for a half-breed slave trader named Mando Gomez to appear. It did not take a mind reader to guess that Herman intended to sell her to the half-breed, who would take her and probably other women south to Apache country.

Nicole had been raped by Herman every day that she had been held in the room and usually again by her guards. Now, with her spirits almost broken, she knew that she must escape soon for once she was sold or traded to Gomez, her fate would be sealed.

The man on top of her rolled off and lay sprawled on the bed. The swine had been drinking whiskey and his words were slurred. "You screw like a corpse, woman," he complained. "But even bad is good."

Out of the corner of her eye, Nicole saw the man's gunbelt hanging over the foot of the bedpost. Attached to the belt was a Bowie knife. That was what she would have to use because the sound of a gunshot would bring men running.

During the seven days of hell she had endured in this room, she had not had a better opportunity than this. Never before had one of the guards drank so much whiskey while being disarmed. "I want to get dressed," she said.

The man grabbed her arm and twisted it painfully. "Not until I say so," he grated. "I may want you again. Stay close."

Nicole swallowed her disappointment and forced herself to lay still beside the man for several more minutes. Then, she said, "Please, I need to use the chamber pot."

"Go ahead," he muttered.

He was in his mid-twenties and his name was Frank. Nicole knew that she was going to either kill him or he would kill her within the next twenty seconds. She got up and reached for the chamber pot she kept under the bed. She was not permitted to take it down the hall and empty it, and the guards were lax about such matters. So when Nicole reached under the bed and slid it out, it was already half full.

The man was watching her closely now, making sure she stayed away from his gun. Nicole gripped the chamber pot in both her hands, and then, in a desperate sweeping motion, she tossed its stinking contents into his face.

He screamed as the urine burned his eyes and blinded him. Nicole's hand darted for the Bowie knife, and when it slid free of its big sheath, she was amazed and momentarily intimidated by its size and weight. But her moment of hesitation was fleeting. As the guard tried to wipe his eyes clear, Nicole drove the knife into his body at a point just under the ribs.

His mouth flew open and his hands fluttered beside his face, which drained white. Nicole fell back in horror and crabbed across the floor to shrink against the wall.

"Goddamit," Frank cried out in blindness as he pitched forward off the bed, "You killed me!"

Nicole covered her eyes and sobbed uncontrollably. Still crying, she struggled to her feet and quickly dressed, hating the fact that she had no clean undergarments. She could smell the men who had used her. It was all she could do to keep from vomiting. She dried her eyes and pulled on her shoes. Then she left the room and ran down the hallway. At the stairwell, she halted and peered down into the lobby to see one of Rod's guards resting on a couch.

Nicole raced back down the hallway to a rear window. It was so filthy that she could not see through the glass, and it was stuck. She pulled off one of her shoes and smashed the glass out, certain that the sound of it breaking would be heard below. But when no one came running up to investigate, she stuck her head out the window and looked down into the alley below. It seemed a hundred feet to the ground, but she knew it was less than fifteen.

Mustering up all her courage, she pulled up her skirt, stuck one leg through and grasped the window frame, not feeling the small shards of glass cutting into her palms and fingers as she dangled for a moment and then released her grip and fell.

She struck the ground hard. She was sure she had broken a leg or ankle until she climbed weakly to her feet. Amazed that she was able to walk, she quickly started to run.

Blindly, not knowing where she was going, only that she should go back north. Back up the trail toward Denver.

Skirts flying, legs flying even faster, she ran through the back streets as she had never run before. When she was finally beyond the town, she began to walk. Her mind was whirling with terrible thoughts. The worst one of them was the thought that they would soon discover her escape and come looking for her. Probably right up this trail.

Nicole looked down at her tracks. Even she would recognize that they were made by a woman's shoe.

She swallowed noisily and left the trail, still moving to the north. Maybe she would come across some good men. Were there any left besides Michael Cotton in this world? Men willing to help save her from a fate worse than death.

Nicole had her doubts until, just as the sun was setting in the west, she stumbled onto Francois drinking wine and eating cheese and French bread. He no longer looked foppish and feminine to her, he looked like a savior.

Nicole came flying out of the underbrush and threw herself into her slightly drunk uncle's arms. They both began to cry.

When Francois could talk, he said, "We have to go back to find Miss Starbuck, Ki, the young doctor and—"

Nicole's face lit up. "Michael is here! He's come for me!"

"Yes."

Nicole wanted to get up and run back to Santa Fe, but reason stopped her cold. "I'm afraid," she said. "Rod and his men will be looking for me soon. We might meet them!"

Francois considered the problem. "Then you stay here," he said, handing her the rifle. "I will go into Santa Fe and find our friends. We will come back for you after we have had our revenge."

Nicole gripped the revolver tightly. She did not want to be left alone, but there seemed little choice. At least, from up here in the rocks, she could see not only her backtrail, but also the main trail leading north out of Santa Fe. And if Rod somehow managed to follow her, she would kill him from ambush and never give it a moment's thought.

"All right," she said quickly. "Saddle your horse and hurry! I will wait here."

Francois stood up. He was a little tipsy and nearly overcome with joy at having Nicole back safe. Never mind that she looked and smelled so bad. He had anticipated such a thing. "I brought you a new dress," he said. "And shoes and underthings. I had the woman at the store pick them out, but I personally selected this."

Nicole's eyes widened as she saw the necklace and earrings. They were matched with jade set in pure silver. She remembered how harshly she had judged this man and was ashamed. "I will never forget this," she vowed. "Never."

Francois nodded. He was too choked up to speak. He touched his niece's cheek and then hurried to saddle and bridle his horse. Just before he rode away, he said, "The pack horse will carry you safely back to Denver. Everything will be all right."

Nicole sat on her knees staring at the new dress and the jewelry. She would take a bath the moment he left her. Then dress and brush her hair. When Michael saw her again, she wanted to look good for him.

Chapter 18

Jessie and Ki moved cautiously down the street. Since Ki had never been seen by Rod Herman or any of his men, he stayed a half step ahead of Jessie.

The Night Owl Saloon was doing a good business. It was the favorite watering hole for rough men who stayed clear of the law. No one asked your name, home town or your business in the Night Owl. When you entered through the swinging doors, every eye in the house turned in your direction. The last lawman foolish enough to enter the Night Owl wearing his badge pinned on his vest had died in less than five seconds, his chest riddled with bullets.

When Ki and Jessie stepped inside, they attracted plenty of attention. The crowd was rough-looking, and Jessie felt their eyes pinned to her bosom. She was about to turn and leave when she heard a chair scrape and a man started to move toward her suddenly.

"That's one of them!" Jessie said, her hand streaking for her gun.

Rod Herman's top gun, the hatchet-faced quick draw artist named Wes, faded to his right and drew his gun with blinding speed. He cleared leather before Jessie and shouted, "Freeze or I'll kill you!"

But he had forgotten Herman's warning about the samurai

and, therefore, did not even realize that Ki was with her. Confident, and with his gun pointed at Jessie, he swaggered forward as several more of Rod Herman's men drew their weapons.

"Well, well," he said. "Have I ever caught me a prize. Get your hand away from your gun, Miss Starbuck."

Jessie stalled for time. "What are you doing?"

"I think you know the answer to that."

"You can't just kill me in front of all these people."

Wes chuckled. "Sweetheart, you're too damn rich and pretty to shoot."

Out of the corner of her eye, Jessie saw Ki reach for a *shuriken* star blade. She released her grip on the handle of her gun and raised her hands. "It looks like you're calling the shots," she said.

Wes smiled. "Damn right I am. But I'll say this much, I've faced men who were not half as quick on the draw as you, Miss Starbuck. Thing of it is, I'm the best."

"Not quite," Jessie said as the samurai launched himself at the gunfighter. His foot came up and broke the man's wrist. Wes's sixgun flew into the air. Then Ki shoved Jessie hard back out the door as the other men hesitated for an instant.

An instant was all that Ki needed as he moved in among them, with his *han-kei* whirling. The two-handled fighting weapon was perfect for this kind of a fight. Connected by a short band of braided horsehair, the two thick wooden sticks were only about seven inches long. But each time they struck, they destroyed flesh and bone. Guns were knocked spinning as the *han-kei* administered its devastation. Wes, his right wrist broken by the samurai's foot strike, was game to the end. With a curse on his lips, he dove for his fallen weapon. He had trained himself to shoot with either hand, and as his left shot forward to grab his sixgun, one of Ki's *shuriken* blades caught his reaching fingers and cut three of them off at the second joint. The gunfighter screamed but still managed to get his bloody left hand wrapped around the butt of his gun. Ki drove one of the whirling handles of his *han-kei* into the side of the gunfighter's face with lethal force. The man collapsed on the floor, bone fragments from his crushed skull driving into his brain.

Jessie jumped back inside the saloon with her gun up and ready. She saw a man behind the bar reach for a double barreled shotgun. "Ki, duck!"

The shotgun roared at the same instant that Jessie fired. Her bullets drove the man backward. He crashed into the back of the bar and sent a shower of glasses and bottles to the floor. Hands slapping at his chest, he slid to the floor. Jessie knew he was dead.

The rest of the men in the Night Owl dove for cover, knocking over and taking refuge behind wooden tables. "Anybody else want a piece of this action!" Jessie demanded.

There were no takers to her challenge. Smoke hung thick in the room. When Michael Cotton and Quentin Daily charged in, the fight was over.

"What took you so long?" Jessie asked.

The two men had no answer as they stared at Rod Herman's men, who—except for the dead gunfighter named Wes—were all writhing on the floor with broken wrists and faces, thanks to the work of Ki's *han-kei*. The samurai was positioned in a crouch, his eyes missing nothing. When he finally did straighten, he grabbed one of Rod Herman's men and dragged him to his feet. "Where are they?" he asked in a quiet and very deadly voice.

The man stared into the samurai's black, unforgiving eyes. "The Santa Fe Hotel," he stammered.

"What room?"

"Upstairs. Room 204."

"Is she alive!" Mike Cotton shouted, grabbing the man from Ki and shaking him in a fury.

"Yeah! I swear she's still alive. At least she was the last time I used—" Too late the fool realized the damning words as Mike's fist smashed his nose into pulp. Ki had to pull the young doctor from the outlaw or he'd have killed him with his bare fists.

"Let's go get her," Jessie said, "what is done is done. Come on!"

Mike realized the truth of her words. He spun around and charged toward the door, yanking his gun out of his holster.

Jessie was right on his heels. She grabbed the incensed young doctor and yanked him completely around. "Are you crazy! If you go storming into that room either you'll get killed first—or second—right behind Nicole. Is that what you want to happen?"

"No," he gritted.

"Then let my samurai go into that room first! He's a fighter, you're a doctor. Use your head."

Ki stood close. When the young doctor looked at him, he said, "I can get inside better and that might make the difference between Nicole's living or dying."

Michael swallowed, and then he seemed to slump. "All right," he whispered. "You go in first. But I mean to be second!"

Ki nodded with agreement. He looked up the street toward the Santa Fe Hotel. When he moved forward, his mind was already on the challenge of getting inside the room without Rod Herman having time to kill the girl.

Rod Herman had gone up to Nicole's room. When he'd found his guard dead and realized that Nicole had killed him and then managed to escape, he'd rushed downstairs and started towards the Night Owl Saloon to gather his men. That's when he had seen Jessie fly back out through the saloon doors and had heard the gunfire. Herman had skidded to a halt and then retreated across the street to hide from view behind the corner of a building.

Minutes later, he'd seen Jessie and three other men come rushing outside and watched as they'd started toward the Santa Fe Hotel. Herman did not have to go into the Night Owl to discover that Wes and his men were either dead or incapacitated. He whirled and ran toward the stable where he had boarded his horse. Saddling in a rush, he rode north toward the outlaw town. He'd done plenty of business there in stolen cattle taken from Ned Cotton's ranch, as well as several other ranchers that had gone out of business.

Herman forced himself to remain calm. After all, the rustler's town was filled with men who would protect him for a price. Men a hell of a lot more capable than the sorry bastards who had just failed him.

Five miles north of town, the fugitive attorney saw a rider fast approaching him. Herman thought nothing of it until, at about two hundred yards, he recognized Francois, the foppish owner of Denver's Plains Hotel. Herman frowned, and then his eyes widened as he saw the hotel owner draw his revolver and bellow some insane challenge in French.

Rod Herman yanked his horse to a standstill and jumped out of the saddle. Very calmly, he drew his carbine from its scabbard. When the charging Frenchman was about fifty yards away and had already emptied his own pistol, Herman took careful aim and shot the man through the heart. The Frenchman made a complete somersault as he went over backward. He struck the earth, rolled over the side of the roadbed and vanished in a shower of loose rock.

Rod Herman jammed his carbine back into his rifle scabbard and mounted his horse. He trotted over to the edge of the roadbed and stood up in his stirrups. The Frenchman's body had rolled half way down the mountainside and it might not be discovered for days. Herman rode over to the Frenchman's horse, which had stepped on its own reins and now stood snorting in uncertain fear. A man on the run never knew when he might need a second animal in case his first mount went lame.

"Easy boy," he said, dismounting and taking his pocket knife from his coat. He sliced one rein away and used the other to control the spooked animal. He remounted and led Francois' horse after him as he continued up the trail. His mind was working feverishly on all the factors working for and against him. Actually, he was not in such desperate shape after all. The only one that could bring incriminating evidence against him was Nicole. And—

A bullet whanged off a boulder almost directly under his mount. The horse reared. Herman grabbed for his carbine again, and when his horse came down, he leaped from its back and led both it and Francois' horse back into the trees with bullets coming at him fast.

Herman forced down panic. He peered around a tree. When another shot came, he had his ambusher clearly in sight. It was a sight that made him grin.

"Goddamn you, honey," he said to himself. "I couldn't have asked for a single person in this world that I'd rather have try and fail to kill me."

Herman checked his weapons. He tied both horses in the brush, and using the forest for cover, he began to flank Nicole. It took him almost twenty precious minutes. When he finally came up behind her in the rocks, he touched her on the back with the point of his carbine. "Surprise," he said.

Nicole spun around. When she saw his grinning face, she reacted with horror. Her own rifle came up, but Herman batted it away and then he smashed her across the head with the barrel of his carbine.

"I'll see you traded to the Apache yet," he vowed, grabbing the unconscious woman and throwing her over one of his heavily muscled shoulders. "But until then, you're my life insurance."

Chapter 19

The death of Francois affected them all very deeply. They'd used two critical hours in tracking down his body and another hour hauling him out of an almost inaccessible canyon. Now they were burying him.

"He was different from anyone I've ever known," Jessie said. "In some ways, an affected dandy, but when it came to honor, courage and integrity, he had more than his share."

Michael said, "I remember how, as a boy, he would always have candy in his pocket when kids met him on the street. He never knew how we used to make fun of his French accent."

It was Ki's turn to speak. "He never confused me with being a Chinaman. Right from the start, he treated me exactly as he did everyone else he held in respect . . . as an equal."

Jessie tossed a handful of dirt on Francois' body which had been wrapped in a saddle blanket. She nodded to the others to begin filling up the grave they'd laboriously carved out of the mountainside. When the burying was done and Ki had planted the simple wooden cross he had carved, Jessie said, "Let's find Rod Herman and Nicole. Let's make sure that this good man did not die in vain."

They nodded grimly and mounted their horses. It was easy to pick up the trail, and they followed it north.

"He's taking her to that secret outlaw town I told you

about," Ki said after the second day. "There's no need to go slow any longer. We might even be able to overtake him on the trail. He's not foolish enough to try to ambush all four of us."

So they rode hard, tossing caution to the wind, intent only on overtaking Rod Herman and his captive before they reached the sanctuary of the outlaw town. After riding almost constantly day and night, they topped a high ridge and Ki shouted, "There they are!"

"And there the outlaw town is," Jessie said pointing to a distant valley where they could see smoke rising from chimneys. "I doubt we'll overtake them, but we have to try."

So they whipped their exhausted horses into a run. The animals responded with courage. They might even have succeeded in overtaking Herman and poor Nicole except that the man glanced back over his shoulder and saw them charging up his backtrail. With a shout, Herman responded by whipping his horse and dragging Nicole's horse along by the reins.

It was a horse race, and the issue was in doubt right up until the last mile when Herman finally managed to reach the outskirts of town with Jessie, Ki, Michael and Quentin right on his heels.

The samurai had his bow ready when he entered the town. He kicked free from his horse and landed on his feet. An outlaw burst from the nearest saloon, and Ki sent an arrow streaking across the street. It buried itself in the outlaw's throat and sent him backpeddling through the batwing saloon doors. Jessie shot another outlaw, and then the fight was on as Michael and Quentin dismounted and took cover under heavy fire.

Jessie saw Herman drag Nicole from her horse. Michael saw it too and went after him, heedless of his own danger. The young doctor was cut down in mid-stride. Before Jessie could move, Quentin Daily was zig-zagging across the street. He grabbed Michael, who was still shooting. With Jessie offering a covering fire, the pair made it to safety.

The samurai had vanished. As soon as the shooting had begun, he'd ducked into the alley. Now, as he burst into the saloon where the greatest concentration of outlaw gunfire was originating, he caught the defenders by surprise. Again, the *han-kei* flashed, and men dropped with bloodied heads. When a man tried to knife the samurai, he found himself crashing through the window with his ribs caved in from a vicious flat-kick to the side.

Ki took the saloon by storm. He was a whirling dervish, a thing almost inhuman. A killing, fighting machine that drove the last terrified outlaws into the street with their hands up in the air calling for mercy.

Ki dashed back into the alley. Moments later, the scene was repeated, and then with a steady volley of gunfire coming from Jessie, Michael and Quentin, the last of the demoralized outlaws surrendered. When they realized that they had been defeated by such a small force, they stood in angry disbelief, those that could still stand.

"Come with me," Jessie said to the samurai. "Michael, bind your own wound, and Quentin, don't let them move. They'll kill you in the bat of an eyelash."

Jessie and Ki hurried down the street toward the hotel where they had seen Herman drag Nicole. "He'll kill her if we try to take him in a rush," Jessie said. "Why don't you go around behind and do what you can."

"And leave you out here under his gun?"

"If I thought there was any other way, I'd try it," Jessie said. "But there isn't. We'll just have to play this out and let the cards fall where they may."

The samurai knocked one of his terrible "Death Song"

arrows on his bowstring. Death Song had a small ceramic bulb fitted just behind the head of the arrow. The bulb had an air hole in it. When Death Song was in flight, it had a shrill cry that could unnerve anyone. Very often, the eerie siren sound of that arrow could freeze an enemy into a moment of fatal indecision. Ki hoped that would be the case today.

Jessie knew that she would be watched from the hotel lobby so she made no pretense of rushing the hotel, but instead, she walked boldly up the street until Rod Herman called. "That's far enough!"

Jessie stopped in her tracks. She saw Herman emerge in the doorway of the hotel, and Nicole was in his grasp. "Let her go and surrender," she said. "This is over."

"Not for me it isn't!"

"Let her go!"

Herman placed his pistol to Nicole's head. "Throw down your gun and come here!" he ordered. When Jessie hesitated, the man cocked the hammer of his gun and called. "I'll count to three. If you aren't walking by then, this woman's brains will paint the door. One . . . two . . ."

Jessie knew she could not wait another second, so she started forward. If Ki did not kill this fiend before she also became his captive, they were lost. The crazed Denver attorney was like a cornered wolverine, and there was nowhere left to hide.

Ki stepped in through the back door of the hotel and moved down the hallway. He saw in a glance that Jessie was almost in Herman's grasp. He raised his bow and fired.

The ominous sound of Death Song caused Rod Herman to twist his head sideways which was exactly what Ki anticipated. Death Song's terrible shriek ended abruptly as its ceramic bulb exploded through Herman's right cheek and then continued on through his mouth to exit out the left cheek and bury itself in the door.

The man was pinned by the face. He tried to scream; failing that, he tried to shoot Nicole, but she managed to break away. Before Herman could begin unloading his gun, Jessie put a bullet through his heart.

The attorney sagged against the door, face still pinned by Death Song. Nicole threw herself into Jessie's outstretched arms and whispered, "I knew you wouldn't stop coming until he was dead!"

"It's over," Jessie said. She looked at the girl and saw the suffering in her eyes. "Michael has been wounded. Not seriously, but I think you'd better get to him right now."

Nicole broke away and flew down the street, still wearing the long, white dress that poor Francois had given her just before his death. She found Michael propped up against a horse trough with his gun trained on the outlaws.

"Oh, thank God you're still alive!" Nicole cried, throwing herself into his arms.

Michael grinned up at Quentin Daily. "This is the girl I am going to marry," he said almost cheerfully.

Quentin Daily nodded with approval. His gun never left the motley gang of outlaws they had captured. "And *these* are the sonofabitches I'm going to see swing from a gallows," he replied with satisfaction.

Watch for

LONE STAR IN HELL'S CANYON

eighty-second novel in the exciting
LONE STAR
series from Jove

coming in June!